THE GROOMSMAN

MARCIA LYNN McCLURE

Published by Distractions Ink
1290 Mirador Loop N.E.
Rio Rancho, NM 87144

Published by Distractions Ink
©Copyright 2018 by M. Meyers
A.K.A. Marcia Lynn McClure
Cover Photography by ©Irina Kharchenko/Dreamstime.com
and ©Volha Kliukina/Dreamstime.com
Cover Design and Interior Graphics by Sandy Ann Allred/Timeless Allure

First Printed Edition: June 2018
First Hardcover Edition: June 2018

McClure, Marcia Lynn, 1965—
The Groomsman: a novel/by Marcia Lynn McClure.

ISBN: 978-0-9996274-7-1

Library of Congress Control Number: 2018950026

Printed in the United States of America

To Mr. Rogers...
The world was a better place when you were still in it!

And to anyone (which is probably everyone),
who has ever been made to feel self-conscious or downright ugly
because of a particular personal physical attribute. You are a
beautiful individual! So help others to know that truth about
themselves too!

PROLOGUE

Madison beamed with prideful arrogance as she introduced the guest she'd invited for supper. "Everyone…this is Pike O'Leary," she presented.

Ambria Blanchard's older sister was radiating such self-satisfaction over the quality of man she'd managed to bring home that Ambria half expected Madison might very well rupture something due to her increasingly ballooning pride.

"And Pike," Madison continued, "this is everyone—Daddy, Mama, Ambria, and Hadley…my whole family."

As their parents shook hands with Pike in turn, welcoming him to the Blanchard home, Madison giggled—not with delight but with triumph. It made Ambria's stomach churn, the way her older sister gloated whenever she brought a date over. Of course, in *this* particular case, Ambria couldn't really blame her sister for being so pleased with herself. Because, when all was said and done, this guy *was* the most gorgeous, beefcaked, super-stud lady-killer Ambria had ever seen in her whole seventeen years of life!

Therefore, she decided she'd allow Madison to get away with her smugness in securing a date with Pike O'Leary—at least for the time being. After all, the dude was at least six-foot-three, with gorgeous dark brown hair, blue-blue-blue eyes, and a flawless, squared jaw that was perfectly complemented by a slight cleft in his chin. He owned an exceptionally straight nose, strong cheekbones, broad, brawny shoulders, and very muscular arms and torso—that much was easy to see, even beneath the navy-blue button-up shirt he wore. His robust dark brows shadowed eyelashes that some might consider wasted on a man—especially when women everywhere were paying three hundred dollars to have a technician attach eyelash extensions to theirs.

Yep, the guy was a gorgeous, muscular morsel who made Ambria's toes curl, literally—she was suddenly aware that her toes were scrunching into curls inside her shoes. And although she wondered how in the world Madison had managed to drag him home for supper, Ambria couldn't fault her older sister's having so much pride in her prize.

"We're glad you could make it, Pike," Steve Blanchard, Ambria's father, said, offering a hand to their guest.

"Thank you, Mr. Blanchard," Pike greeted, shaking her daddy's hand with firm confidence.

"So," Ambria's little sister, Hadley, began, stepping up to stand directly in front of Pike, "you're Madison's newest boyfriend, huh?"

Ambria felt humiliation for her family's sake and sympathy for their guest too—for as calm as he appeared, she could sense he was uncomfortable with Hadley's question. Still, Hadley was eleven, and even though she'd managed to learn to brush and style her own hair before school in the morning, she was still struggling with permanently implanting any sense of tact into her middle-school character.

"Well, I…uh…she, uh…Madison invited me for supper, and I accepted her invitation, so I'm not sure that I'm…um…really her…" Pike stammered.

Ambria grinned. Golly! The guy was even more mouth-watering when he was embarrassed.

"My heck, Hadley!" Madison playfully scolded her youngest sister. "Pike and I are just friends, and I thought he'd like to have supper here tonight, bein' that Mama *is* making red stuff and noodles and everythin'." Gazing up into Pike's fine-looking face, she blushed, apologizing, "You'll have to forgive Hadley, Pike. She thinks every guy I bring home is already my boyfriend, you know?"

As one of Pike's dark brows arched with what Ambria silently translated—*How many guys do you bring home?*—she smiled. At least the guy appeared to be wising up faster than most of Madison's victims. Ambria figured she better get every eyeful of the spectacular supper guest she could, for she was pretty certain that by the time Pike O'Leary sat through one entire hour with Madison at supper—well, Ambria would never see him again, that was for sure.

As Madison then returned her attention to Hadley, glaring at her with a threatening expression communicating that her baby sister, as well as Ambria and their parents, would pay for Hadley's tactlessness once supper was over and her guest had gone home, Ambria placed a protective, comforting arm around her little sister's shoulders to reassure her.

"Well, why don't we just dive right in, hmm?" Ambria's mother, Erica, inquired. "We're just so happy to have you tonight, Pike." Looking to Ambria's daddy, her mama added, "Isn't that right, Steve?"

"Yep," Steve Blanchard agreed with a firm nod and a friendly smile. "I always enjoy havin' company for supper. I like to show off what a good cook my wife is."

Ambria smiled when her father gently swatted Erica on the bottom, triggering a delighted giggle from her. She kept smiling as she followed everyone else to the dining room. If there were one thing Ambria knew her father did *not* enjoy, it was company—for supper or for any other reason. In fact, the entire Blanchard family, with the exception of Madison, was die-hard introverts. Madison was the black-sheep extrovert, who always seemed energized and raring to go to any social gathering. Ambria, her mama, daddy, and baby sister enjoyed being social, doing stuff with friends and family—but afterward always felt vamped, completely drained of energy. It was something Ambria hadn't understood or even realized for a long time—the fact that she liked to be out and about with people as much as Madison did but always felt like she needed a nap afterward, while Madison ever and always asked, "What next, guys?"

Ambria had been feeling down on herself all summer. Oh sure, she knew that teenaged girls were always engaged in a seemingly endless battle with low self-esteem. And she understood that Madison was older than she was—already beyond that part of her life and full-throttle loving her second year in college with confidence. But all summer long, Ambria had been troubled by Madison's having seemingly endless energy and joy, while Ambria didn't.

And then, a few days before her senior year of school started, Steve Blanchard had noticed the worried expression on his middle daughter's face and inquired as to what was bothering her. Ambria felt ridiculous confiding to her father that she thought something was physically wrong with her—that she might have an unseen illness or something like slow carbon monoxide poisoning—because she didn't feel as delighted in socializing or as animated afterward as Madison did.

"Well, that's because you're like me, baby," her father had answered. "I like people as much as the next guy, but they wear me out, you know? Emotionally more than anythin'. And that doesn't mean that I don't like hangin' out with them or that I'm weak. I just process things differently...and you do too." He'd pulled Ambria to sit next to him on the sofa, put a strong, loving arm around her shoulders, and added, "And that's absolutely normal and absolutely fine." He placed a kiss on her temple and continued. "Think of it this way. You and Madison each have an imaginary purse with you. Now when Madison wakes up in the mornin', her purse is empty. But with each interaction she has with a person or people throughout her day, it's like somethin' is dropped directly into her purse—a twenty-dollar bill, a wallet, a cell phone, makeup. So when Madison comes home at the end of the day, her purse is full of all kinds of stuff that makes her happy. You, on the other hand—you wake up in the mornin', and your purse is already full. You've got all your happy stuff in there—lip gloss, money, photos. But throughout the day, whenever you interact with someone, *you* give *them* somethin'. You give one person your wallet, another person your twenty-dollar bill, another person your lip gloss...so that by the time your day is through, your purse is empty, and you have nothin' left to give away. It doesn't mean you're not social or not fun or that you don't enjoy being with people. It's all about how you energize, how you fill your imaginary purse. Madison fills her purse by being social. She gains energy from it. You fill your purse by hangin' out at home, listenin' to chill music, readin', writin'. That's all it is, baby; it's the way you fill your purse, the way you reenergize, as compared with the way Madison fills hers. And each way is the right way for each of you individually. I'm like you. If I had a purse...well, it's totally empty at the end of the day. But then I come

5

home to my family, a delicious supper your mama has made; I read a book, stretch out on the couch, snooze a bit, and I'm recharged. Do you see what I'm sayin'?"

Ambria nodded, feeling much better about herself. "I do, Daddy. That makes a ton of sense." She smiled at her daddy, leaned over, wrapped her arms around his middle, and hugged him. "So I guess I can stop worryin' that I've got carbon monoxide poisonin' or somethin', right? I'm just boring."

"No," Steve Blanchard responded firmly. "Well, yes," he corrected. "Yes, you can stop worrying about carbon monoxide poisonin'. But no, you are *not* boring. In fact, a lot of introverts are the ones who keep the social functions excitin'. They just expend every ounce of their energy doing it." He paused a moment, his handsome, middle-aged brows puckering with concern. "You don't think *I'm* boring, do you?" he inquired.

Ambria giggled, reassuring, "Not at all, Daddy. Don't be a dork."

He chuckled, hugged her more tightly, and concluded, "Well, see? You're not boring either, Ambria. You're far from it. You're just not Madison."

Oddly enough, her father reminding Ambria that she was *not* Madison gave her even more comfort. Truth be told, Madison Blanchard was a stinker ninety percent of the time, and Ambria liked knowing that she most likely was not.

As everyone sat down at the table, Ambria noted the way Madison made certain only she sat next to Pike. In fact, Hadley and Ambria exchanged knowing glances as they watched Madison offer Pike the chair perpendicular to her father's at the head of the table, promptly sitting down in the seat right next to Pike—the seat that was usually Ambria's.

"Just sit across from us, Ambria," Madison dictated to Ambria, gesturing to the seat across the table from Pike—the seat that was usually Madison's.

"And I'll sit here," Hadley announced, plopping down in the seat between Ambria's and perpendicular to their mother's. "Since you're sittin' in my seat, Madison," the tactless eleven-year-old added.

"Thanks, Hadley," Madison said, forcing a fake smile. "It just works out better this way…because Pike can be nearer to Daddy in case they want to have some guy talk durin' supper."

Ambria glanced to Pike then, her cheeks catching fire as she saw that *he* was looking at *her*—grinning at her—as if he knew exactly how peeved she was with Madison's contriving.

She offered an awkward smile to him in return, and when he winked at her, expressing further understanding, the butterflies that erupted in her stomach took her breath away. Glory hallelujah, the man was dazzling in his magnificent, fine-looking hotness! Once more, Ambria wondered how on earth Madison had managed to net this Pike.

Then again, Madison herself was a very pretty young woman. And when the green-eyed natural blonde with the perfectly proportionate figure chose to be, she could be almost fatally charming! Still, something about the air of sincerity that hovered around Pike O'Leary hinted that a pretty face did not easily take him in. So why was he there, sitting next to Madison? It was indeed a conundrum.

Hadley leaned very close to Ambria then, whispering, "Wow! Madison must've really turned on the voodoo to snag this guy, huh?"

Ambria bit her lip to keep from giggling as both she and Hadley looked up to see Madison spitting daggers their direction. Fortunately for them both, Pike was involved in light conversation with their father and hadn't heard Hadley's comment.

"Here we are," Erica announced as she entered the room with one large serving bowl in one hand and another smaller one in the other. "I hope you like our red stuff and noodles, Pike. It really is our family's favorite."

"It looks great, Mrs. Blanchard," Pike said, his voice as deep and rich as the molasses Ambria's mama used for the muffins waiting to go with the red stuff and noodles.

"Had, will you run and get the ginger muffins please?" Erica asked her youngest daughter.

"Of course!" Hadley exclaimed, jumping up from her seat. "Want me to get the broccoli too?"

"No, I'll get that. But do grab the butter for the muffins, okay?" her mama replied.

"It really *is* red," Pike said, studying the saucy red stuff in the smaller serving bowl.

"Yes," Madison verified. "It's really good too. Mmm! Tender pieces of beef, and Mama simmers it in the sauce for hours. It's not a marinara sauce, and it's not a barbeque sauce. It's way different."

As Ambria's mother returned, setting a bowl of steaming broccoli on the table—Hadley placing a basket of ginger muffins and a butter dish nearby—Pike asked, "So, Mrs. Blanchard, did you invent the recipe?"

Erica giggled. "You're wonderin' why it's called red stuff and noodles instead of somethin' fancier, right?" Pike nodded, and she continued, "Well, it started out as a recipe for a simple Hungarian goulash I'd found in a cookbook a million years ago when Steve and

I were first married. But the original recipe was so mild the first time I made it that I just kept addin' more or less of certain ingredients, completely eliminatin' a few things as well, until it became red stuff and noodles. I mean, I suppose it's still Hungarian goulash, technically. But we call it red stuff and noodles because that's what the girls called it when they were little. They'd always ask me to make it for their birthday suppers. 'I want that stuff…that red stuff with noodles,' Ambria told me when she was four." Erica smiled and shrugged, adding, "We just started referrin' to it as red stuff and noodles after that. And now I guess you'd call it an heirloom recipe…with a plain-Jane sort of name."

"Well, it smells great," Pike commented as Erica took her seat at the end of the table. "And the story that goes with it makes me even more eager to try it."

Ambria's smile broadened as her mother blushed a little, delighted by the young man's compliment.

Once her father had said a blessing on the food, he picked up the large bowl of steaming, extra large egg noodles and used the accompanying tongs to plop a heaping helping of the pasta right in the center of his plate.

"And don't be shy, Pike," Steve instructed. "Erica always makes enough to feed an army, so eat what you want and as many servin's as you stuff down, okay?"

"Thank you, sir. I don't mind if I do," Pike said as Steve passed the noodles bowl and tongs to him. "Madison has been talkin' up this red stuff and noodles thing to me for weeks, so my taste buds are primed and ready."

Ambria looked to her mother, who was wearing a rather smug, knowing grin, as if understanding had just dawned on her. Arching one brow conspiratorially, she winked at Ambria. Yep, now they both understood why Madison had been begging Erica to make red stuff and noodles for supper every day for two weeks straight—so she could win Pike O'Leary over with her mother's cooking!

"So," Steve began as he ladled the red sauce over his noodles, "I'm assumin' Madison knows you through school." Steve handed the bowl to Pike, and he accepted. "Do y'all have a class together or somethin'?"

"Yes, sir," Pike answered with a nod. "Madison is in my sociology class this semester."

"Sociology class, hmm?" Steve mused. "Do you mind if I ask what your course of study is?"

"Of course not," Pike assured, passing the bowl to Madison. "I'm working on my criminal justice degree, specializin' in forensic science."

No one, including Ambria's father, who had posed the question, commented on Pike's answer. He paused, looking around at the wide-eyed faces of the Blanchard family.

"Did…did I say somethin' wrong?" he asked, obviously unsettled.

"No, no. Of course not," Madison reassured him. "They just…I mean…they just…"

"Madison's never brought a smart guy over for supper," Hadley offered. "She usually only brings home guys whose college classes are all weight liftin' and stuff like that."

"Oh," Pike said, nodding, grinning, and obviously very amused by Hadley's truthful answer.

"Hadley," Madison growled through clenched teeth.

Misunderstanding her sister's irritated reaction, Hadley quickly added, "But you're really awesome, Pike—because you're smart *and* you have the big muscles Madison likes on guys. You know?"

Pike chuckled as Madison's cheeks proceeded to turn from pink to crimson to outright blood red.

"Well, I'm glad you think my planned career path makes me sound smart, Hadley," Pike offered. "I guess I've got somebody fooled, at least."

Ambria could see Madison's teeth clenching and unclenching. Hadley had managed to prick at her temper. Ambria silently prayed that Madison wouldn't lose her cool in front of their supper guest. Then again, the naughty part of Ambria wondered if it wouldn't be best in the end—for Madison to show her true colors, thereby sending the handsome Pike O'Leary running out of the house, screaming in terror at the realization that Madison had almost snagged him in her web.

Of course, Ambria instantly felt guilty for thinking such a thing. Madison wasn't that bad—not deep down inside. Ambria's mama and daddy were constantly reassuring Ambria and Hadley that Madison would turn out all right in the end—turn out to be a really nice person.

Still, there were times Ambria wondered whether her parents were trying to reassure Madison's sisters during such conversations—or themselves.

"Well, Hadley's in sixth grade, and of course, it's obvious Ambria's still in high school."

Madison's mentioning her name drew Ambria's attention back to the supper conversation and away from her own musings.

"Although Ambria is a senior this year," Madison was saying to Pike. Madison exhaled a breathy, lilting laugh then before adding, "Although with that rack she's sportin', you'd think she was already twenty-one and waitin' tables at Hooters or somethin', wouldn't you?"

As everyone at the table stopped chewing—stopped breathing, in fact—Madison added, "I mean, really…what a freak, right? What other girl do you know who's only seventeen and has bigger boobs than her own mother?"

The silence was more than merely just awkward: it was palpable, deafening in its shrieking silence.

For her part, Ambria dared not look up—not to glare at Madison nor to mutely look to her father or mother for help. It wasn't like she wasn't used to Madison's criticisms—especially at times when Madison's temper flared. She was hideously used to them. But this time was different; this time Madison had made fun of her in front of a stranger—a man—a gloriously good-looking man. Even so, Ambria was determined to appear strong, to give the impression that Madison's comments rolled off her back like water from a duck's feathers.

But it was true. Ambria's bra size was bigger than her mother's, as well as Madison's, and it was the thing she was most self-conscious of. In everything that could be cruel in the life of a teenager, Ambria's bosom was what she hated most. No matter how many times people told Ambria how pretty she was—complimented her on her perfectly perky nose, lovely hazel eyes, dimpled cheeks, and cinnamon-brown, auburn hair (as her mother referred to it)—all Ambria could do was hate her bosom. Not that a 34C bra was anywhere near the freakish size Madison accused it of being—but when her mama and older sister barely plumped out size B cups and Ambria had been wearing a C cup since sixth grade—well, Ambria simply hated her buxomness, and her older sister knew it.

"Madison," Ambria heard her father rather growl in an irritated voice.

"Well, it's true, Daddy," Madison stated. "I mean, look at her! She's a freak of nature with those things."

"Madison!" Erica scolded then.

Yet the true champion of Ambria's tattered self-esteem came from an unexpected source then.

"This red stuff and noodles is absolutely as good as I've been hearin'. Even better!" Pike O'Leary said, reaching to the center of the table and retrieving a ginger muffin from the basket. "And I hope you don't mind if I have another one of these babies, Mrs. Blanchard."

As Ambria ventured a glance upward and across the table, it was to see Pike wink at her teary-eyed, frustrated mother with unique perception. He then put a hand on her father's shoulder and said, "No wonder you like to show off your wife's cookin', Mr. Blanchard. I swear to you, I've never eaten anythin' like this before...ever."

Ambria understood at once. Pike discerned not only that Madison's dig at her little sister was grossly inappropriate but also that the family's discomfort was extreme. He knew the matter should be addressed once he had gone home—privately, without an audience.

"Um...yes," Ambria's father stammered. "Erica makes a mean meal...every time."

Ambria felt her father's hand squeeze her knee with reassurance, and he looked at her, his eyes narrowed and his ears red with the anger he was holding at bay. Ambria knew that there would be hell to pay once Pike had taken his leave after supper, and it would be Madison that would have to pay it.

Nevertheless, even though she knew Madison would get a verbal lashing the likes she'd never known from their mother and father, Ambria was a wreck inside. Sure, she smiled and pretended to be okay, involving herself in the supper conversation and being as kind to Madison as she could manage. But inside, she was sobbing with sadness, embarrassment, and frustration. How could Madison make light of the thing that upset Ambria most in front of company? How could a sister be so cruel? Ambria couldn't conceive how anyone could even think of being so cruel. The concept was so foreign to her natural character that no amount of reassurance from her father about introverted versus extroverted personalities could ever ease the emotional pain and misery her sister had put her through that night.

"I'm sorry, Ambria," Hadley said in a quiet whisper. "It's my fault she got mean. I'm so sorry."

"It's okay, Had," Ambria whispered in return. "And it's not your fault."

"Hadley," Erica reprimanded, a reminder that it was not polite to whisper at the table.

"Sorry, Mama," Hadley mumbled. And yet in the next moment, she whispered to Ambria again, "And don't worry about your boobs, Ambria. Madison is just jealous of them. Personally, I hope that my boobs end up being like yours. I am a little worried right now, though, because even though mine are starting to show more, my right one is a lot bigger than my left one. Can you imagine what Madison will do to me if I end up having two different sizes of—"

"Hadley…that's enough," Erica quietly scolded once more.

"Sorry, Mama," Hadley said.

Ambria grinned. She could always count on Hadley to cheer her up—even if most of the time Hadley didn't know she was doing so.

Thanks to her little sister, Ambria made it through the rest of supper without having an emotional breakdown over what her older sister had done.

Still, as her mama left, heading toward the kitchen to retrieve the cake she'd made for dessert, Ambria glanced across the table to see Pike looking at her. His gaze was so blue, blue, blue—so blue it was disconcerting. She could see the pity in his eyes—the sympathy he held for her because of what Madison had done—and she couldn't take it any longer.

"Daddy," Ambria began, "I'm so full I don't think I can manage dessert. And besides, Chunk hasn't had his walk today. May I be excused?"

As always, her father thoroughly understood Ambria.

Smiling with empathy, Steve said, "Of course, sweetie." Then he turned his attention to Pike, adding, "Our dog, Chunk…well, let's just say if we don't walk him at least once a day, he starts to look like his name."

Pike smiled and looked back to Ambria as she pushed her chair back. Standing, he offered a hand to her across the table, saying, "It was really nice to meet you, Ambria. Thanks for havin' me over."

Ambria grinned, knowing she was blushing with delight as she took his hand.

"Thank you for comin'," she offered as he held her hand a little longer than necessary—held her hand in his large, warm, strong, callused hand. Goose bumps prickled her arms at the insanely awakening sensation of his touch.

"Well, don't forget who invited you to supper in the first place, mister," Madison laughed. "It wasn't Ambria, you know."

"I know," Pike said, still smiling at Ambria—still clasping her hand. "Have a nice walk with your dog, okay?"

"I will, thanks," Ambria assured him. She felt disappointed—cold and lonesome somehow when Pike released her hand.

"You're not havin' cake, sweetie?" Erica asked as she entered the dining room again, carrying dessert.

"I couldn't eat another bite, Mama," Ambria said. "And besides, Chunk needs his walk."

Erica nodded emphatically as she agreed, "Oh, indeed he does. You see, Pike, if we don't walk our dog, Chunk, very regularly...he starts to resemble the meanin' of his name."

Pike chuckled. "That's what I hear."

As she started to leave the room, Ambria glanced one last time to the gorgeous, beefcaked, super-stud lady-killer. Oh, what she wouldn't give to gaze at that man forever.

"Bye," she said. "It was nice to meet you, Pike."

"Nice to meet you too, Ambria," Pike O'Leary returned in his deep, molasses-rich voice.

"Come on, Chunk," Ambria called as she hurried toward the front door. "Let's go for a walk."

She smiled when the middle-aged red wheaten Rhodesian ridgeback came galloping into the front entryway.

"There's my baby," Ambria soothed in baby talk as she scratched Chunk behind the ears. As she clipped his leash to his collar, Ambria ventured one last glance into the dining room, desperate for a final glimpse of Pike O'Leary. She blushed when, to her astonishment, she found he was still standing and looking over his shoulder at her.

Bye, she mouthed, thrilling when he smiled and nodded to her.

"Come on, Chunk," she sighed. "Let's walk off another meal of Madison meanness, okay?"

♥

Parked just a ways down the road from the Blanchard home, Pike sat in his beat-up, old, canary-yellow Mustang, still stunned by what a piece of work Madison Blanchard had turned out to be. She'd seemed so nice when they were in sociology class—always smiling, kind, and friendly. Then when she'd begun telling him about the meal her mama was making—the red stuff and noodles—well, being a starving college student living in an efficiency apartment, Pike had jumped all too eagerly at accepting Madison's supper invitation.

But wow! The way she had lit into her little sister that way, making fun of her—making fun of her body even. Pike had been so shocked—so instantly angry and perturbed—he hadn't been quite sure that he could continue to sit there and play nice to Madison. Pike had three sisters of his own, and he knew how fragile a girl's self-esteem was and how body conscious they were in their teens— and beyond.

"What a hustlin' canine she turned out to be," Pike grumbled to himself, putting the cinnamon toothpick he'd been chewing on in the trash bag lying on the passenger seat. Reaching into his shirt pocket, he retrieved another cinnamon toothpick—he'd gone through three already while waiting. Pressing it to his tongue, Pike exhaled a sigh of thorough disgust with himself. He should've seen through Madison long before he found himself at her family's supper table. He shook his head, knowing it was the lure of a good home-cooked meal that was his undoing. He was just so tired of eating canned and frozen food that he'd tumbled.

"It's obvious she's just jealous of her sister," he mumbled aloud. And it was true! Oh, Madison Blanchard was pretty enough—even hot by most guys' standards—even guys he knew who *had* standards.

But her little sister Ambria one-upped her in every regard. And not just in looks but manners too. Ambria hadn't said too much during supper, even before her fanged sister went after her. But he'd watched her carefully—seen the sincere kindness Ambria showed to Hadley, her parents, and even Madison the *Canis familiaris*. Ambria Blanchard was the jewel of the family—Pike knew it. Her warm, kind of golden-brown eyes were filled with a ton of secreted emotion and intellect. But Madison had made certain Ambria's confidence didn't wax too strong. And she'd probably been making certain of it for Ambria's entire life! Pike could not leave, knowing he'd never see Ambria Blanchard again, without offering at least a little pep talk to her, a little reassurance as to why her older sister was so cruel to her—envy.

And then, sure enough, the half an hour of sitting in his car was about to pay off—for he saw Ambria and Chunk walking up the sidewalk toward the house—toward him. Pike noted how pretty the girl was, liked the way the Rhodesian ridgeback pulled her along with him instead of the other way around.

Getting out of his car, Pike whispered to himself, "I really do need to get a different car. I look like a teenager in this thing."

Pushing the Mustang's driver's side door closed, Pike called, "Hey, Ambria!"

Ambria looked up, smiling when she saw him coming toward her. Pike figured her smile was a good sign—hoped it meant she was feeling better about her big sister's malice.

"You're still here?" Ambria asked as she walked toward him—as he strode toward her.

"Yeah," Pike said, shoving his hands in his pockets as if he were in eighth grade instead of twenty-one and working on his BA.

"I would've thought you'd have been long gone by now," Ambria giggled. "After havin' had to endure that gag-thering tonight."

Pike grinned. "Gag-thering...that's funny," he chuckled. "But, uh...I wanted to say somethin' to you."

"Okay..." Ambria said. She looked scared to death all of a sudden—as if she half expected him to bite her head off.

"First of all, this will most likely be the last time we ever see each other," he began, "considerin' the fact that I don't plan on ever speakin' to your sister again, let alone bein' any kind of friendly with her."

"You don't?" the girl inquired—her delicate, perfectly shaped eyebrows arched in surprise.

"Nope," Pike affirmed, shaking his head. "The way she treated you in there..." He paused, shaking his head again, renewed disgust fresh in his mouth. "That was bad."

Ambria shrugged. "Well, I'm sure she didn't mean to..." she started.

"Don't defend her, Ambria," Pike said. Reaching out, he took hold of her shoulders, stared directly into her golden-brown eyes, and said, "It was completely uncalled for...and a personal attack. And I'm sure you know why."

Again Ambria shrugged, even for Pike's firm grip on her shoulders. "Well, it's just how she is. I...I..."

"It's wrong," Pike interrupted. "And I know it's none of my business, but I feel like someone outside of probably your parents should tell you that Madison is just jealous of you."

"Jealous of me?" Ambria squeaked, obviously disbelieving.

Pike was distracted for a moment, thinking on how much he liked the sound of her voice—the soft, rather soothing sound of her voice.

"Yeah...jealous," he assured her at last. "You're way prettier than she is, and I'm sure she feels threatened by you...in a lot of ways. So when she thinks you might be winnin' over someone's attention, she lashes out and tries to make you look bad in front of them."

Pike O'Leary paused, grinning an entirely provocative grin as he said, "I mean, Hadley is right. I'm not a muscle-bound gym-type. I've got a brain. Maybe Madison really isn't used to guys that can see through her shi...stuff."

Ambria was breathless as she realized what he was saying. In truth, Pike O'Leary was telling her that *she*, Ambria Blanchard, was prettier than Madison! And he'd thought enough of her to wait until she and Chunk got home before leaving—thought enough of her to tell her she was prettier—to tell her Madison was just jealous and that was why she was so mean.

"I mean, it's not my place at all," Pike noted aloud. "It's your family business. But I just couldn't leave without tellin' you that, although I would never be so rude to your daddy and mama, or so disrespectful of your home, I about came unglued when Madison pulled that shi...shenanigan. And I just wanted to make sure, before I left, that you knew, from someone outside your family, that she's just jealous."

Pike frowned then, took the toothpick out of his mouth, and flicked it into the street.

"And don't let her get away with that anymore either," he grumbled. "She's a bully. Don't let her do it. Your boobs are perfect, and your little sister is right: Madison is just jealous because you have a better body…uh…figure than she does. So don't let her get away with that shi…stuff anymore, okay?"

Ambria sighed, entirely bewitched by his charming chivalry. Oh, what a man—gorgeous as well as smart, perceptive, and thoughtful! And he had the muscles too, whether or not he was a gym guy.

"Thank you, Pike," Ambria managed in a voice barely above a whisper—for her gratitude to him, her tender emotions, were beginning to well to the point she knew tears would fill her eyes at any moment. Sure, he'd said her boobs were perfect, and most people would consider that highly inappropriate at the very least of it all. But to Ambria, it made his encouragement all the more sincere and wonderful.

"That really does mean more to me than you can ever know. I mean, I love Madison…but she can be very difficult to get along with," Ambria admitted. "Thank you for recognizin' that…and for stickin' around long enough to tell me. It means more than you know."

Pike shrugged broad, broad shoulders, retrieving two toothpicks from his shirt pocket.

"Well, I'm serious. And even though you don't know me, I hope you'll take what I have to say to heart and think about it if Madison ever tries that shi…stuff again, okay?" he told her. He popped one toothpick in his mouth, offering the other to her with, "You want one? They've been soaked in cinnamon oil, so they can be a little spicy."

"I do," Ambria said, somehow finding the courage to reach out and accept the toothpick. She touched it to her tongue and at once hummed, "Mmm!" as the delicious flavor of cinnamon filled her mouth.

"Well...I gotta get home," Pike sighed. He seemed fatigued all at once. "I've got homework." He smiled at her, adding, "Be sure to tell your mama and daddy thanks again for me, okay? They're awesome people. And your mama really is a great cook. I haven't had a meal like that in a long time."

"I'll tell them," Ambria assured him. All at once she felt like bursting into tears for the fact he was leaving, in knowing she would never see him again. Still, she held fast to her emotions—remained steady.

"Thanks," Pike said. Then, exhaling another sigh, he said, "Maybe I'll see you around."

"Maybe," Ambria mumbled.

He turned, walked back to his car, slid into the driver's seat, and, once the engine roared to life, pulled away from the curb and drove away.

As tears spilled from her eyes—tears over the cruel way Madison had treated her at supper, tears that a gorgeous man had given her the pep talk of her life, and tears in knowing she would never see him again—Ambria hurried Chunk back to the house.

Once inside, she unlatched the leash from Chunk's collar, called, "I'll be on the computer," to her family, and hurried into the den.

Even as she listened to her parents chewing Madison out, again, Ambria tried to ignore their conversation. Instead, she headed straight to the college digital yearbook page, grateful that Madison never signed out of any site she was ever logged into.

Quickly she typed *Pike O'Leary* into the search bar, smiling even as she brushed tears from her cheeks. For there, looking back at her from the computer monitor, was a portrait of Pike. Of course, his course of study and hometown info accompanied it, but it was his photograph that Ambria was focused on.

Right-clicking on Pike's photo, Ambria sighed with relief when the "save as" option came up. Quickly she saved his image into her personal documents. Resizing it to the approximate size a wallet school photo might be, she printed it, snatching it from the printer and closing her document before racing up the stairs to her room.

Still weeping over the fact she would never have the chance to be with, talk with, and touch the man who had given her a sudden push in the direction of a bit more self-confidence, Ambria grabbed the craft scissors she kept in her desk drawer and began to carefully cut the excess paper from around Pike's image.

"Maybe every day my purse gets pillaged and I come home emotionally wrung out," she mused to herself, "but no one can ever take this away from me."

Then she hid the photo in the little pocket behind her driver's license in her wallet. Determined never to forget what Pike had told her—determined never to let Madison get away with bullying her or humiliating her ever again—Ambria slipped Pike's photo from its hiding place. She studied it for a very long time, and the longer she looked at it and thought of the fact that a man like him thought she was prettier than Madison, the more confident she felt.

"Perfect boobs, huh?" she whispered as she slipped Pike's picture behind her driver's license once more. And for the first time since the fourth grade, Ambria didn't feel sick to her stomach about the size of her bra and what was in it.

CHAPTER ONE

"What do y'all think?" Harmony asked.

Ambria smiled with admiration—felt tears brimming in her eyes as her joy for her best friend's happiness welled to a crescendo. Harmony and Charlie were so perfect for one another! And even though Ambria knew the coming week before the wedding on the following Saturday would be beyond busy, she was too happy to worry about it.

"Yowza, Harmony!" Kayla exclaimed. "Seriously…you look like ya just stepped right out of *Vogue* bridal photo spread!"

Ambria giggled with agreement. "Yes, ma'am!" she further assured. "Charlie is goin' to go bananas when he sees you walkin' down the aisle toward him in that gorgeous white gown. It's perfect!"

Harmony exhaled a heavy breath of relief and smoothed her long dark hair, reassured by her friends' approval. "It is perfect, isn't it?" she sighed as she studied herself in the mirrors of the Carolina Jasmine Bridal Shop. "I figured this will probably be the only time in my life that I'll actually get to wear somethin' so beautiful, so I went with the mermaid cut and the V-neck. And I love, love, love the sweep train, don't you?"

"Mmm-hmmm," Ambria agreed in unison with Kayla.

"The lace overlay is so beautiful, Harm," Ambria added. "And that gorgeous sable hair of yours, when it's all gathered in an updo…oh, it really is perfect for you!"

"Thanks," Harmony sighed with delight, still studying herself in the mirrors.

Large patterned scrolling and flowers over sheer white, the lace was the crowning glory of Harmony's wedding dress—and suddenly Ambria was even more impatient for Harmony and Charlie's wedding day to arrive!

"They sure did a great job with the alterations, Harm," Kayla noted. "It really does fit like a glove."

"Yes, they did," Harmony agreed.

"I picked up my dress yesterday, and it fits perfectly, as well," Ambria offered.

"Mine too," Kayla said. "Now if I can just keep from gainin' even one little ounce before next Saturday…"

"Oh, I hear that, Kay," Ambria giggled. "One ounce is all it would take for me to split the side seams of my dress, and I'm not exaggeratin'."

"Oh, you two stop," Harmony playfully scolded. "Your bridesmaid dresses are not that fitted."

Ambria exchanged amused glances with Kayla. "Are you kiddin', Harm?" she asked. "When you said you wanted us all to wear mermaid-cut dresses to coordinate with yours, I had no idea they'd be so tight just above the knee! We'll be walkin' around like…like…"

"Like fish outta water…well, mermaids outta water, that is," Kayla finished.

"Oh, y'all quit exaggeratin'! They're not that tight," Harmony giggled. "And you know you like them. And be honest…don't you just love all the sequins? And the tulle skirt at the bottom?"

"You mean the tulle fin at the bottom?" Ambria teased.

Harmony laughed, "Oh, just admit it, Ambria. You'll love bein' a beautiful, sparkly, seashell-pink mermaid!"

"Yeah, Ambria," Kayla confirmed. "At least you're the maid of honor so you get to wear the seashell-pink dress. The rest of us have to wear the seaweed-green ones."

"They're asparagus green, Kayla, and you know it," Harmony scolded with a loving wink.

"I know, Harm," Kayla admitted. "And I do love my dress! I'll confess, I'm excited to be a mermaid for one day."

"Me too," Ambria maintained. "Even if the fin on the bottom of my dress will have me walkin' around in baby steps like I just got my legs."

"You'll look gorgeous, baby steps or not!" Harmony exclaimed, clapping her hands together with delight. "Oh! And I want to give you two one of your bridesmaid gifts a bit early."

"Harmony…" Ambria began to argue, as the bride-to-be hurried behind the changing screen in the mirrored fitting room. She was so uncomfortable when it came to receiving gifts. All her life Ambria had enjoyed giving gifts whenever and to whomever she could. But receiving them—well, she simply wasn't good at it, at least not by the world's standards. Whenever someone gave Ambria a gift, the mingled emotions of joy, excitement, and a sensation of feeling unworthy rinsed over her. Furthermore, unlike her older sister, Madison, Ambria wasn't the sort to shriek with delight or jump up and down with displaying her pleasure. Ambria received gifts with her heart—the tenderest part of her heart. Therefore, although she was grateful for any gift of any kind, it was an emotional experience for Ambria and one that couldn't be expressed with what she perceived as an overreactionary display. Receiving a gift was difficult for Ambria, even and especially when the gift meant so much to her.

Still, Harmony knew that about her best friend. After all, Harmony and Ambria had been bosom friends for almost fourteen years—since the day they first met at Irish step dance class when they were six years old. Yep, Harmony Carolina Fumm—soon to be Harmony Carolina Oaks—knew Ambria better than anybody else outside her immediate family. And so when Harmony returned with two asparagus-green gift bags topped with bunches of mermaid-blue and asparagus-green gift tissue paper, Ambria's anxiety in knowing she was about to receive something lessened a bit. Harmony knew Ambria well, and therefore she would know that Ambria loved the gift, even if she didn't jump up and down squealing with delight the way Madison would have.

Handing one gift bag to Ambria and the other to Kayla, Harmony began, "So…the house Daddy and Mama rented for the attendants to stay at this comin' week has a gorgeous—and I do mean gorgeous—pool out back. And since I want everyone to have the time of their lives next week leadin' up to the weddin', even if we'll all be as busy as a moth in a mitten with weddin' stuff, I saw these bathin' suits online and just had to, had to, had to get them for y'all." Wagging an index finger at Ambria, she added, "And no squirrelin' out of swimmin' because you're still bashful about your body, Miss Ambria Blanchard! After all, you have the best body of any of us, and I want you havin' fun in the pool along with everybody else."

Ambria rolled her eyes, shaking her head as she marveled at how truly Harmony knew her. It was true. The moment Harmony had mentioned a swimming pool, Ambria had thought, *Oh no!* to herself. No amount of reassurance and encouragement had ever driven her self-consciousness about the size of her chest from her mind. Even after Madison had finally quit teasing her about her bra size several years before, the first thing Ambria saw when she looked into any mirror was her boobs.

"See?" Harmony giggled. "I knew it! You're already worryin' about playin' in the pool." Harmony shook her head. "Ambria, you and I wear the same size in everything, you know. And you don't see just my boobs comin' at you when I'm walkin' toward you, now do you?"

"No, Miss Harmony, I do not," Ambria answered with teasing sarcasm.

"Then there you go," Harmony affirmed, gesturing toward the gift bag she'd just handed Ambria. "I am marryin' the man of my dreams and havin' my Mt. Pleasant, South Carolina, dream weddin', and I want everyone to be as happy as I am! So you will swim, Ambria Blanchard, and you will have the time of your life...got it?"

"Yes, ma'am," Ambria giggled. Yet as she pulled the tissue paper out of the gift bag, reached in, and removed the bathing suit inside, her confidence began to wane again.

"Oh, I love it, Harm!" Kayla exclaimed after removing her own suit from its gift bag. "It's gorgeous. I love the sequins!" Kayla clutched the suit to her chest with glee, adding, "And it's blue. I love the blue!"

"Oh, good grief, Harm," Ambria moaned. "If it ain't bedbugs, it's ticks with you every time! You expect me to wear this? In front of other people? Why, it looks like somethin' you'll be wearin' for Charlie on y'all's weddin' night."

As both Harmony and Kayla giggled in argument, Ambria shook her head and continued to study the lovely, and well-intended, gift from her friend. Oh, there was no denying it was gorgeous! The beautiful blue sequined bathing suit had wide shoulder straps and side cutouts. Oh, she was grateful that the bottom of the suit was not French cut and incorporated a cute little built-in ruffled skirt. And she was likewise appreciative that the top of the lovely one-piece had extra, but not obvious, bust support. But it was the side cutouts, moderate as they were, that freaked her out.

"What? Is this supposed to take the attention off my freakishly big ol' bazoombas and focus it on my flabby waist sides?" Ambria asked, giggling.

"Flabby waist sides?" Harmony and Kayla exclaimed in unison.

"You're the one with the twenty-inch waist!" Harmony pointed out.

"*36-24-36...what a winnin' hand*," Kayla sang, quoting the Commodore's classic song, "Brick House." "Only you've got a ridiculously small, twenty-inch waist, Ambria."

"I bought one for myself too, Ambria," Harmony began. "And other than the fact that I don't have your puny waist, it's very flatterin'." Again Harmony pointed a scolding index finger at Ambria. "And you're wearin' it with all the rest of us, and you're goin' to have the time of your life, you hear me?"

Ambria smiled, nodding with promising to do as Harmony wished. After all, it was Harmony's dream wedding to her dream man. And as the maid of honor, Ambria wanted to make sure as many of her best friend's dreams came true as possible. Therefore, if Harmony dreamed of having all the bridesmaids and groomsmen splashing around in a swimming pool together, then Ambria would make sure they did.

Glancing up to the wall clock, Harmony gasped and exclaimed, "Oh, swat my hind with a melon rind! If we don't hurry, we're goin' to be late for supper."

"Ah yes, the supper," Kayla sighed, winking at Ambria. "How could we forget."

How could they forget indeed. The "meet-and-greet" supper had been rather haphazardly thrown together just that morning. It seemed men liked to wait until the very last minute to do anything that had to do with wedding planning—at least, men liked to wait until the very last minute if Harmony's fiancé, Charlie, were any man to measure the fact by. The man had waited until just four nights before—only twelve days before the wedding—to settle on his final list of groomsmen. Thus, the supper that Harmony, Kayla, and Ambria were at risk of arriving late to would be the very first time the male and female attendants of Harmony and Charlie's wedding had ever met with one another.

"Oh, hush, Kayla Mae Griffith! Every one of Charlie's friends is tall, dark, and handsome, just like he is," Harmony assured as she began to struggle to get out of her dress.

Ambria hopped up from her seat and unzipped the beautiful mermaid gown at the back.

"You know I wouldn't let any one of you girls have a groomsman escort you who was crass and ugly," Harmony offered.

"I just don't understand why we haven't met them all before now," Kayla posed. "I mean, this really should have been all sorted out a long time ago."

31

Harmony exhaled a heavy sigh as Ambria helped her out of her wedding gown.

"Oh, I know, girl. But it's just men, that's all," Harmony began to explain. "Charlie hasn't said as much, but I know he just hates all this fuss. If he had his way, we'd just march over to the preacher's house on a Monday evenin' and get hitched that way. So in order to save my lover-man a lot of unnecessary stress, my very wise mama suggested that I give Charlie the very minimum of responsibility that I could…which I did. Still, he certainly did come in with his list of six groomsmen by the skin of his teeth, didn't he? I mean, I could've had ten or fifteen bridesmaids if I had wanted to—although that would've been ridiculous. Still, I figured choosin' six groomsmen would be fairly easy for my boy. Only, you know how he is—so private, with a small circle of friends. In fact, two of his groomsmen are his younger brothers, so I didn't think it would be too hard for him to choose four more. But I guess it was. We didn't sit down and match bridesmaids and groomsmen up until late last night. So we both figured a supper tonight would be the best way to get everyone together."

"Well, you're a better bride than I would be," Kayla laughed. "I'd be pullin' my hair out over him waitin' so long."

"Oh, me too," Ambria agreed. Carefully Ambria placed Harmony's mermaid wedding dress on the lavender chaise lounge nearby and then helped Harmony unlace the corset she was wearing beneath.

"Well, in truth, it made all this weddin' nonsense more enjoyable for me, knowin' Charlie could take his time on his part," Harmony admitted. "Otherwise, I would've been far too distracted with makin' certain he wasn't miserable with all the plannin' to enjoy it myself. He's such a darlin', and I've seen too many grooms be far too miserable to do that to my lover-boy." Harmony laughed to herself, and the smile on her face reiterated to Ambria how truly her friend loved Charlie.

"Well, even though I'm glad Charlie's avoidin' the stress of the weddin' as much as possible," Kayla began, "I hope you're not matching me up with some little teenager brother of his, Harmony. I'd feel ridiculous bein' paired with a juvenile the way Chelsea was at her sister's weddin'. That was preposterous, if you ask me...pairin' up a twenty-year-old woman with a fourteen-year-old brother of the groom." Kayla paused a moment, arching one eyebrow with mingled curiosity and disgust. "Why, is that even legal? I wonder."

Harmony shrugged, answering, "I don't know. But neither of Charlie's brothers is that young. Tanner is twenty-one, and Caleb is nineteen, almost twenty. So you'll be fine, Kayla."

But Kayla grumbled, "Nineteen...still has 'teen' in it."

Harmony laughed as she slipped off her white heels and reached for her shorts. "Well, we didn't pair you with Caleb, Kayla. Or Tanner either. So you can breathe easy."

"How about me?" Ambria pried. "Am I takin' one for the bridesmaids' team and bein' coupled up with the 'teen' brother?" Although she was willing to do anything Harmony asked of her to ensure the wedding went off with as few hitches as possible, Ambria silently prayed she'd at least be linked to Charlie's brother Tanner. At least he was her age and not younger than she was.

Harmony laughed and pulled her blouse on over her head. "I told you that everyone will meet their other half for the weddin' at supper. So quit jawin' on about it, and let's get goin', hmmm?" Pulling her hair up into a ponytail, she added, "Let me tell Miss Charlotte that we're finished in here so she can get my dress into a bag for me. I'll pick it up later. Y'all just run out to the car. I'll be there in a minute or two."

"A real minute or two, Harm?" Ambria asked. "Or an estimated minute or two?"

Harmony rolled her eyes. "A real minute or two. I promise," she answered.

As Harmony hurried off to find the woman who did alterations at the bridal shop, Ambria exchanged amused glances with Kayla.

"Looks like we'll be late for supper after all," Ambria laughed.

"Looks like we will indeed," Kayla agreed with a smile.

Ambria and Kayla had both been pleasantly surprised when Harmony had joined them in the car mere minutes after she and Kayla had arrived. Ambria was relieved about the fact too, for it was nerve-wracking enough to have had to wait until a week before the wedding to find out who Charlie's best man would be—who her escort as Harmony's maid of honor would be.

"I hope the guys didn't get stuck in traffic," Harmony said as Ambria parked her car—a banged-up dark cherry Kia Spectra that was starting to show its age of thirteen years—in the parking lot of Mancini's Italian Restaurant.

"Well, it's only five, so hopefully they missed it," Ambria reassured.

"Oh, wait! There's Charlie's car right over there," Harmony noted, pointing to the far side of the parking lot.

"Well then, let's get the awkward introductions over with," Kayla sighed from the backseat.

Ambria could've sworn her stomach had jumped up into her throat as she followed Harmony into the restaurant.

"Prepare yourself, honey," Kayla said from just behind her. "I can't imagine that all of Charlie's friends are as sweet and handsome as he is. Let's keep our fingers crossed that Harmony's not exaggeratin'."

Ambria grinned, feeling sorry for any of Charlie's groomsmen who weren't up to the very high expectations of Ambria's fellow bridesmaids. After all, Kayla was right—Charlie Oaks was a very good-looking man! The epitome of "tall, dark, and handsome," Charlie was the kind of man that made every woman turn her head to take a second, third, and even fourth look when he walked by. Percentage statistics were certain to prove that it was inconceivable there could exist six tall, dark, and handsomes that were close enough friends to be attending the same wedding. Charlie's brothers were indeed good-looking, like Charlie himself. But that still left four groomsmen who just might not measure up to what Kayla and the others were expecting.

As for Ambria, she and her daddy had had a conversation several months before about the fact that, as her daddy phrased it, "There are an awful lot of ugly and average-lookin' people in the world. Not every man can scoop up a young woman as pretty as you, Ambria…or as good-lookin' as that Charlie Oaks your friend Harmony is marryin'. There just aren't enough pretty people to be had."

"Daddy!" Ambria had playfully scolded. "Everyone in the world is beautiful!" She shrugged, admitting, "I mean, naturally not everyone can be as glamorous as Harmony and Madison, or as handsome as you and Charlie. But I think the word 'ugly' is awful mean, don't you? And most of us are as plain as a pine plank but beautiful all the same…on the inside, at least, right?"

Ambria's father had chuckled, put his arm around her shoulders, and agreed, "You're right, baby. How about we say that there are an awful lot of homely and plain-on-the-outside people in the world, hmmm?"

Ambria had laughed and hugged her father—more for referring to her as pretty than for softening his view of homely or plain people.

And now, as she followed Harmony into Mancini's, looking up and smiling when she saw Charlie gesturing to join him in a private dining area off to one side of the restaurant's entrance, Ambria determined that if there were a less-attractive-than-Charlie man in the groomsmen lineup, she hoped it was his best man, so that she could treat him with the kindness and respect he deserved. Guiltily she also thought to herself that perhaps if Charlie's best man weren't *People* magazine's Sexiest Man of the Year, then she might not stand out as the plainest plank of the bridesmaids. After all, Kayla, Jordan, Brooke, Sierra, and Chelsea were all glamorous, gorgeous, and true archetypal South Carolina belles. And although Ambria liked hair and makeup as much as the next South Carolinian girl, she didn't feel nearly as confident as they all did—preferring to be the last one to enter a room, thereby avoiding attention.

In fact, true to her nature, as Harmony hurried into the private dining area, Ambria stepped aside, motioning for Kayla to precede her.

"Ambria Blanchard! You have got to get over this bashfulness," Kayla scolded, even as she moved past Ambria and into the dining room in front of her.

As she watched everyone greeting one another—for Harmony, Kayla, and herself appeared to truly be the last to arrive—Ambria took a deep breath, exhaling slowly.

It had already been a long day. Work had been more demanding than usual. Ambria was the creative director at Miss Woodhouse's Tearoom, and she had to make certain that everything was in order for the seven consecutive serving days she would be missing due to Harmony's wedding and the festivities leading up to it. It had been an exhausting task, work responsibilities alone had emptied her analogous purse, and she worried she wouldn't have enough gas in the tank, so to speak, to meet and mingle with her friends, let alone meet six new people.

Yet straightening her posture with determination—and also in knowing she would enjoy the time with the good people in her life—Ambria stepped into the private dining area.

"Over here, Ambria!" Harmony called at once. "You're sitting here, next to the best man!"

"Okay," Ambria said, heading toward the table. As she approached, she could see that the seating had been arranged so that Charlie was at the head of the table and Harmony at the other end across from him. As she watched Brooke sit down next to Caleb Oaks, Ambria was reminded of Harmony's talent at making certain everyone was happy. After all, Caleb was Charlie's youngest brother as well as the youngest groomsman, and Harmony's younger sister, Brooke, was still a teen as well—at eighteen, a teen even younger than Caleb's nineteen.

"Right here, darlin'," Harmony said, pulling out a chair for Ambria.

"Oh no, Miss Harmony," a deep, masculine voice said then. "Allow me to do that. After all, if we're to be connected at the hip for this comin' week and the weddin', I best be a gentleman at least."

"Thank you," Ambria said as she allowed the man standing behind her to seat her at the table.

She hadn't looked at the man yet—at Charlie's best man—afraid he would be disappointed to see that Harmony's maid of honor was not as flamboyant a Southern belle as his friend's bride.

But when she saw him take his own seat next to her—carefully eyeing him peripherally—she was wildly disconcerted when she felt goose bumps breaking over her arms. Although she had not had a good, solid look at him, she could sense he was very handsome. His voice alone revealed he was—the deep, rich nature of it. In truth, his voice made her feel—well, it somehow whisked her back— whisked her back four years, bathing her in memories of another supper and a voice she'd heard that night—a voice as deep and rich, as warm and wonderful as molasses taffy.

"It seems we cross paths again, Miss Ambria Blanchard," the man said.

And she knew then. Ambria knew that the voice and the man were not simply similar to the voice and the man that had changed her life four years before—but that the same man himself was sitting next to her.

Thinking of the worn photograph she still cached in a secret space in her wallet, Ambria turned and nearly fainted with euphoric shock when she found herself gazing into the blue, blue, bluest eyes of the most gorgeous, beefcaked, super-stud lady-killer she'd ever seen.

"P-Pike O'Leary?" she stammered in a whisper.

"Well, fancy meetin' you here," he chuckled, smiling at her— smiling the same dazzling, alluring, provocative, downright seductive smile that had lingered in Ambria's memory for the past four years.

CHAPTER TWO

"What's it been? Four years?" Pike asked Ambria.

"Um, yeah...I think so," Ambria stammered in response. Holy smokes! He was so gorgeous! More gorgeous than even she remembered—more gorgeous than the four-year-old photograph still secreted in her wallet. Everything about Pike O'Leary seemed more gorgeous—his shoulders broader, his eyes bluer, his voice more bewitching. He was incredible!

Suddenly his nearness and the overwhelming physical effect it was having on her caused Ambria to begin to panic—panic about the existence of his photograph in her purse. After all, what if he found out it was there? What if he guessed? In truth, Ambria had continued to carry Pike's picture because it had been a sort of talisman to her—sustaining her in times when her self-confidence was low. Sure, she'd met him once. Sure, she never in a million years would've thought her dreams would come true and she'd see him again someday. But the pep talk he'd offered the night he'd come to supper as Madison's guest four years before had been a powerful thing for her, and she'd clung to it, and not just his photo, ever since.

And now, although the logical part of her brain silently assured her that there was no way Pike could know about her secret, treasured photograph of him, the freaking-out part of her brain convinced her to hide her purse under her chair as quickly as possible just in case he had X-ray vision like Superman. And so she did—removed her purse from her lap, plopped it on the floor, and pushed it under her chair with her feet.

"How is your family?" Pike inquired.

"Oh! They're all…just great. Madison is fine. She actually runs a flower shop in downtown Mt. Pleasant," Ambria offered.

"And everyone else?" Pike continued to urge. He chuckled, adding, "Your little sister was awesome that night…so unguarded and sayin' exactly what she was thinkin'. I loved that."

"Well, Hadley has a little more tact nowadays, and we're all very relieved that she does," Ambria explained, smiling. "And Mama and Daddy are just dandy." She shrugged, feigning calm. "Everyone's just fine."

"I'm glad to hear it," Pike said, nodding. "And?"

"And what?" Ambria ventured.

"And? What about you?" he pressed. "How have you been?" He smiled again. "I mean, obviously you're a maid of honor at the moment."

Ambria tried to keep the nervous giggle tickling her throat from escaping, but she failed. "Oh yes…I suppose I am. And…and obviously you're a best man at the moment."

Still staring at her with his blue, blue, bluest eyes, he said, "It's a funny old world, ain't it? I mean, you and me, meetin' up again, and under such circumstances as this."

"Y-yeah," Ambria managed.

"Are we all to understand that you two already know one another?" Harmony asked from her seat at one end of the table.

"We do indeed," Pike responded. "Ambria and I met about four years ago…under difficult circumstances. Isn't that right?" He winked at Ambria, and she felt butterflies begin dancing in her stomach.

"Yes, we did," Ambria managed.

"Difficult circumstances?" Harmony prodded.

"Yep," Pike began, still staring at Ambria. "I had a class with Madison, and she invited me to supper with her family one night."

"Madison invited you?" Harmony mumbled.

Ambria's felt a blush rise to her cheeks. She knew Harmony would put it all together any second. After the evening four years before when Madison brought Pike to supper and had been so cruel to her—after Pike had given Ambria his pep talk—Ambria had confided the entire story to her best friend, Harmony. Nevertheless, she had never mentioned the name of her knight in shining armor, and she'd never shown Harmony the photo of Pike she kept in her wallet either. She'd wanted to keep that part as her own—his name, his photo.

But Harmony's eyebrows arched in realization as Pike continued.

"Yeah, she did. Madison had been telling me about her mama's red stuff and noodles for forever, and I caved in and accepted her invitation to supper with their family."

Ambria knew the identity of the mysterious, heroic supper guest of four years ago was no longer her secret; Harmony knew now too.

"Ohhhhh!" Harmony drawled, smiling with full understanding. "So *you're* the guy." Glancing at an already blushing Ambria, Harmony quickly added, "You're the guy that Madison couldn't sink her talons into. Ambria told me about that."

"Yep, I had a narrow escape that night, I guess," Pike agreed. Instantly, however, he seemed to realize how harsh the comment might have sounded to Ambria, Madison's sister. "I mean, Madison was a wonderful girl...just not my type."

"Well, Madison is actually much better now," Harmony assured Pike. "In fact, she's doin' all the flowers for our weddin'. Isn't that right, Ambria?"

"Yes, she is," Ambria answered. "She's an incredible florist." She dared to allow her gaze to linger in the alluring blue, blue, blue of Pike's fascinating eyes, adding, "And she *is* a lot different now. Much kinder, less self-absorbed."

Pike's smile broadened, and he reached out, brushing a strand of hair from Ambria's cheek. "Well, I'm glad to hear that."

Ambria's entire body was riddled with goose bumps at the feel of even the slight touch he'd gifted to her.

"Well then, I guess everyone has officially met their significant other for the weddin'," Charlie announced. "I say we eat! Then we can talk details about the upcomin' nuptials after, right?"

Harmony smiled, winked at Charlie, and agreed, "Yes! Let's feed these men first. I surely do not want to talk weddin' particulars with a bunch of *hangry* men!"

Being that they had probably been waiting just outside the door to the private dining area—no doubt eavesdropping in hopes of hearing their entrance prompt—two waiters stepped into the room and, beginning with Harmony and Charlie, began taking meal orders.

Pike could not stop staring at Ambria! *Yo-ho-ho!* he thought. For the woman Ambria Blanchard was even more attractive than she had been as a teenager!

Pike tried not to be too obvious as he studied her pretty face and copper-cinnamon hair—as he carefully perused her appearance from the top of her lovely head to the tips of her cute little flip-flop-clad toes. But in truth, he'd never had a harder time yanking his attention away from anyone or anything in his whole life!

Furthermore, he was driven to engage her in conversation. He could not have cared less about ordering a meal; he just wanted to know more about Ambria, know everything about her.

"So," Pike began forthrightly, "are you goin' to school? Workin'? What all have you been up to since I saw you last?"

Ambria blushed, and Pike felt his heart actually leap a little inside his chest.

"I…um…I went to college a couple years, but when my dream job opened up about three years ago, I jumped at the chance to snag it," Ambria answered. She shrugged her shoulders—which Pike was *sure* were rose-petal soft beneath her cute little green blouse. "I found it kind of too stressful to go to school and work full time…" She shrugged again. "So I followed my dream and have been happy that I did ever since."

"And what dream job were you able to procure?" he pressed, feeling sort of desperate to know every little thing he could find out about absolutely everything about her.

Her blush deepened, and again Pike's heart leapt in his chest. He found it a strange, uncomfortable, even kind of disturbing sensation. But he knew it was a good thing. No other girl had ever caused it to happen to him—not in his whole life.

"I work at Miss Woodhouse's Tearoom here in Mt. Pleasant," she said. "My official title is creative director, but basically all I do is come up with the theme and ideas for the tearoom every month and see to the little details, you know?"

"Wow, it sounds very…very, um, what's the word…Victorian?" Pike said, smiling at her.

She giggled, and it had the same fascinating effect on him that soft rain on an autumn day did.

"It *is* very Victorian," she acknowledged, giggling again and making Pike feel like he was sitting on an old wood bridge, watching the fall leaves drift from overhead to go sailing away in a babbling brook. "At least the décor of all the tearooms are. You know, each little private nook and even the larger areas are Victorian in atmosphere. Even the tearoom for children." She sighed with delight, adding, "I really do love my job."

"Not a lot of people can say that," Pike mentioned. "And it sounds awesome. I mean, girly and all, but awesome—like somethin' my mom and sisters would really like."

"Well, if they like anything Victorian, English bone china, tea—especially our herbals! They are divine!—and good teatime food, they would love it," she assured him. "This month's theme is *The Secret Garden*, and it's one of my favorites. The menu is extraordinary!" She paused, adding, "In truth, I'm disappointed that I'm goin' to miss a whole week of teatimes next week. I do so love to see people enjoyin' our tearoom."

Pike's smile was as broad as a barn door; he could feel that it was. But there wasn't a thing he could've done to tone it down, even if he'd wanted to. Ambria Blanchard was something else! Furthermore, it said a lot about her love for her career when she could catch a dude up in the wonder and anticipation of a Victorian tearoom.

"How about you?" Ambria asked, jostling Pike from his musings over how perfectly charming she was.

"Uh, me?" Pike asked.

Ambria giggled as she nodded, because he looked completely confused for a moment, as if he'd been daydreaming or something.

"Yes," she assured him. "What do you do? I always thought maybe you'd become a spy or somethin'...like a Jason Bourne type."

He chuckled, shaking his head and saying, "Nope. Nothin' so excitin' as that." He winked at her, adding, "Too much travel required, you know?"

Ambria laughed, amused at his expression—as if he were getting ready to tell her he had an embarrassing sort of job. Still, she guessed she'd kind of set the bar high by admitting to him she'd thought he'd become a spy.

"I'm actually just a forensic science technician," he divulged. "A criminal scene investigator. You know, the people who take all the gory photographs and bag up all the nasty blood, hair, and bodily fluids at a crime scene?"

Ambria's eyes widened. "Seriously?" she couldn't help but ask.

"Seriously," he chuckled. "Although it's not like they make it out to be on TV and in movies. I do a lot of lab work and photographin'. That's pretty much what I specialize in...the photography part of it."

Ambria's mouth dropped agape in admiration. It seemed that Pike O'Leary put the sociology class he'd had with Madison in college to good use.

"Wow," she breathed. "I'm kind of in awe of that."

Pike puffed an amused laugh. "Oh, believe me, I know for a fact that what you do is far more impressive. Comin' up with ideas for a place like you work..." He shook his head with admiration. "I'm tired just tryin' to imagine it. Too much creativity and imagination required for what you do."

"Are you ready to order, miss?" one of the waiters asked, startling Ambria from her focus on Pike.

"Oh, um…yes," she stammered, trying to remember what it was she ordered almost every time she was at Mancini's. She had a favorite—but was still so overwhelmed with the fact that Pike O'Leary in the true and living flesh was sitting right next to her, she couldn't remember what was even on their menu.

Finally, in order to buy herself some time to gather her wits, she said, "I'll have ice water…and no lemon, please."

"Ice water, no lemon," the waiter repeated. "And what else, miss?"

At last Ambria's brain shifted out of the ditz zone, and she answered, "The spinach salad to start. Just half, please."

"And for your entrée?" the waiter kindly urged.

"Just spaghetti and meatballs," Ambria finished with a sigh. "I love y'all's spaghetti and meatballs."

"Oh, me too," the waiter agreed. Turning to Pike then, he said, "And for you, sir?"

Ambria gritted her teeth for a moment, frustrated with herself. How on earth could she have lost her mind enough to forget that ninety-five percent of the time she ordered half a spinach salad and spaghetti and meatballs at Mancini's? Mancini's had been her favorite restaurant since it first opened when she was a kid, for pity's sake!

Still, as she watched Pike order his meal—listening to his smooth, rich voice as he spoke—she figured any woman would probably forget her own name when she was the subject of his attention. "Ambria," she actually whispered out loud to herself, wanting to make certain she hadn't lost her mind completely.

"What's that, miss?" the waiter asked.

"Oh, nothin'," she assured the twenty-something Mancini's employee. "Just tryin' to remember somethin'."

"And you wanted the full spinach salad, sir?" the waiter asked Pike.

"Yes. And I'll have the spaghetti and meatballs, as well," Pike ordered. "I kind of have this thing about Italian restaurants I've never been to before," he said, looking back to Ambria. "I have to try their spaghetti and meatballs before I try anything else—you know, check out the basic dish."

"Me too!" Ambria giggled. "It's like I want to see how much effort they really put into their sauce and meatballs, you know?"

"I do, exactly," Pike agreed.

"Well then, you'll both be well pleased tonight," the waiter assured them. Ambria finally noticed his nametag—*Mike*. "Ours is honestly the best I've ever had."

"Me too," Ambria agreed.

"Wonderful," Pike said, handing his menu to Mike.

"I can take your menu if you're finished, as well, miss," Mike offered to Ambria.

"Oh! Oh, of course," Ambria said, handing him hers.

"Thank you. And your salads will be out shortly," Mike assured them as he turned his attention to Brooke and Caleb. Until that moment, Ambria hadn't even realized they were sitting next to her.

"Now, where were we?" Pike inquired, leaning toward Ambria as he rested his elbow on the table. Again the butterflies in Ambria's stomach let themselves be known—for it was as if Pike were calculatedly blocking everyone else's view of her.

As she watched Ambria and Pike sit in such rapt interest and conversation with one another, Harmony's heart swelled with elation! She could see the light in Ambria's eyes—the radiant light of wonderment. Furthermore, she could see the delight, the interest, the pure bewitchment in Pike's eyes as he stared at her friend. Oh, what divine intervention had found its way into their wedding party.

Glancing up to where Charlie sat at the head of the table, she smiled at him, slightly nodding in the direction of Ambria and Pike. She smiled wide to indicate to him that she was excited about what was transpiring between their two best friends. Charlie understood at once—being that he and Harmony could already communicate perfectly to one another without any words being spoken—and nodded his approval.

Harmony's excitement grew as her thoughts lingered on the sure knowledge she'd only just gained—that Pike O'Leary had been the man to change Ambria's life four years before—that he was none other than the "gorgeous, beefcaked, super-stud lady-killer," who had come to supper with Madison, only to leave having given Ambria a new outlook on herself. He'd pointed out Madison's jealousy of her younger sister and told her never to doubt herself again—or something to that effect. As Ambria's best friend and most trusted confidant, Harmony had seen, firsthand, the self-confidence, self-assurance, and strength Pike's attention, encouragement, and compliments had gifted Ambria that night, and she instantly loved him for it. She shook her head in disbelief, for it was no short of a miracle that Harmony and Charlie's best friends would prove to have such a history together. And in that moment, Harmony made a decision. Oh sure, the upcoming week and Saturday would be about her and Charlie—about the prep and fun for their wedding. Nevertheless, it was obvious that heaven itself had a purpose for making certain Ambria's and Pike's paths crossed

again, and Harmony meant to make sure they stayed crossed—
forever!

♥

Ambria tried to swallow the disappointment that began to rise in
her chest as the bridesmaids and groomsmen began to leave the
table in the private dining room at Mancini's. Oh, how she'd loved
being with Pike—sitting next to him, steeped in entirely private
conversation. He'd hardly talked to anyone else at all during the
course of dinner, not even Harmony. His attention had been totally
Ambria's for the taking, and she'd taken it. But now, dinner was
over, the details of what everyone needed to do during the
upcoming week concerning the wedding had been discussed, and
Harmony's and Charlie's closest friends were starting to leave.

Yet Ambria didn't want her time with Pike to end. He was
wonderful, engaging, quick-witted, kind, interesting—not to
mention delectable to stare at. She still couldn't believe he was there,
sitting next to her—that he would be her escort for the wedding.
Merely seeing him again had been a dream come true, a dream she'd
dreamt for the past four years. And to anticipate being near him for
the entire coming week—why, she was giddy with anticipation. But
she still didn't want him to leave her right then—or ever.

"Well, I'd better be gettin' home," Pike said, rising from his seat.
"I've got one more day of work to trudge through if I hope to have
the entire upcomin' week off for the weddin' festivities."

He took hold of the back of Ambria's chair, pulling it out for
her as she stood.

"Thank you," Ambria said politely.

"Oh, it was my pleasure, Miss Blanchard," Pike said. He was
smiling down at her when she turned to face him.

Noting that everyone else had already left or had begun to leave the room and were now bunched up by the exit, Ambria found her courage to say what she'd been hoping she'd get to say to Pike O'Leary for years.

"And thank you for that night four years ago, Mr. O'Leary," she offered in a quiet voice. "For takin' the time to say what you did to me, for carin' about my feelin's, and…and just encouragin' me. You'll never know what that meant to me…to my life."

Pike's smile faded a bit, and he glanced away a moment with discomfort. "Well, you deserved a lot better than you got that night from your big sister," he admitted. "And I just couldn't leave without makin' sure you knew it." His smile broadened, and he added, "I'm pretty flattered that you even remember that."

"Oh, I remember it," Ambria told him. She realized that the only reason she'd found the courage to tell him what she'd just told him was *because* of him—because of the courage he had planted inside her the night he'd come to supper for red stuff and noodles.

"I've always remembered it," she continued. "Remembered that if a guy like you could find me worth talkin' to that night—tell me such kind things and encourage me the way you did—then I must be worth somethin' after all."

Again Pike's smile faded a little, as if he were embarrassed or somehow slightly disappointed. Ambria's smile grew, however, as she watched him reach into the front pocket of his black button-up shirt and remove two toothpicks.

"Well, if a girl like *you* remembers me at *all*, to be honest, I'm gettin' pretty swell-headed," he chuckled. "Want a cinnamon toothpick? They're kind of hot, bein' that they've been soaked in cinnamon oil." His smile broadened, and he winked at her. "Still, I figured if you could handle one four years back, you oughta be able to handle one now."

He placed one toothpick on his tongue, holding the other one out to her.

"Oh, I loved them!" Ambria assured him, accepting the toothpick. "Although I'm not sure how Harmony will feel about her maid of honor walkin' around with a toothpick hangin' outta her mouth."

"Aw, she's too busy makin' eyes at Charlie to notice," Pike assured her. He glanced up at the way everyone else was still bunched up at the exit. "Looks like they're off like a herd of turtles," he chuckled. "But I gotta get back. Four a.m. comes much faster than I would like to admit."

"Well, drive safely home," Ambria said. The taste and sensation of the cinnamon-oiled toothpick in her mouth felt wonderful, and she knew it was because Pike had given it to her.

"I will," he promised. "Are you headin' home? I'll walk you to your car."

Ambria's heart sunk with a thud to the pit of her stomach when she realized she was Harmony and Kayla's ride home. Glancing to the doorway, it was obvious neither one of them were ready to leave yet. Therefore, she was going to miss the opportunity of a lifetime.

"I...I have to wait for Harmony and Kayla," she explained with aching disappointment. "We all came together in my car."

"Well, I'm sure I'll have another chance this comin' week, hmmm?" he sighed with exaggerated discontent. "But you make sure Charlie or somebody walks you girls out, promise me?"

Ambria nodded, totally enchanted by his caring manner.

"Well then, I'll see you soon," Pike said.

"See you," Ambria said.

Yet Pike paused a moment before taking his leave. His blue, blue, bluest eyes narrowed as he studied her for a moment.

"I still can't wrap my head around it," he said. "Me and you meetin' up like this. Our best friends are gettin' married. It's like it's fated, right?"

"Yeah. It is," Ambria agreed.

"Well, in that case," Pike said.

A quiet, euphoric gasp rocked Ambria as Pike removed the toothpick from his mouth and leaned down, placing a firm, quick kiss to the corner of Ambria's mouth that did not secure her own toothpick.

Rising to his full stature, he grinned, put his toothpick back in his mouth, and said, "I wasn't about to miss that opportunity again." He winked. "Now you get home safely, all right?"

"A-all right," Ambria breathed.

"Bye now," Pike said as he turned and strode toward the herd of turtles bunched up at the exit. "I'll see y'all later," he said as he pushed through the dilly-dallying group. "*Some* of us have to work for a livin', you know."

As Ambria watched him go—as she listened to everyone saying their goodbyes to him—her knees went weak, and she plopped back down into her chair.

Her mouth was on fire because of the cinnamon toothpick—but her lips were on fire from Pike's quick, yet intensely affecting, kiss.

"Pike O'Leary?" she whispered to herself. "Really?"

After all, it did seem like a dream—all of it. But it wasn't a dream. It really had happened! Pike O'Leary was Charlie's best friend. Pike O'Leary would be Ambria's counterpart in every aspect of the wedding. Pike O'Leary—the man she'd met only once before, the man who had changed her life—she would see him again during the coming week. It was a fantasy come true!

"All right then," Harmony said, hurrying over to Ambria, taking hold of her arm, and pulling her to her feet. "Let's get on home! You've got a pot of beans to spill, girl! A big ol' pot of Pike O'Leary beans! So let's drop Kayla off, and then you're comin' with me. 'Cause from what I just saw, you've got a piece of hot co'nbread to go with them beans!"

"You have no idea," Ambria said as Harmony linked arms with her.

"Well then, you best fill me in," Harmony giggled as she and Ambria pushed through the herd of turtles still stacked up at the exit. "Come on, Kayla, let's go." Harmony paused only to kiss Charlie and say, "I'll see you in a couple of hours, baby. Me and Ambria have a few weddin' details to go over."

"All right, sweetie," Charlie said.

"What's the rush?" Kayla asked, hurrying to catch up to Harmony and Ambria. "And, Ambria, did I see Charlie's best man kiss you just now?"

"Um, yes…we…uh…we've met before," Ambria admitted.

"Well, I should hope so!" Kayla exclaimed. "The two of you were like two little lovebirds all cuddled up and nestin' durin' supper. A body woulda thought the rest of the world had shriveled up and died, leavin' nobody but the two of you left, the way you two were huddled up."

Ambria smiled, sighed with pure euphoria. For what Kayla had said was true: Pike O'Leary had hardly said three sentences that weren't meant for Ambria during the whole of supper. She bit down hard on the cinnamon toothpick in her mouth, causing a deluge of cinnamon oil to flood her mouth.

"Pike O'Leary," she whispered to herself. "Good glory be."

CHAPTER THREE

As Ambria sat at the supper table with her family, her thoughts were again drawn to Pike O'Leary. Not that she'd quit thinking of him for even one whole minute during the past twenty-four hours since being with him at Mancini's the night before. But sitting there with her family just as she had four years ago when she'd first laid eyes on the gorgeous, beefcaked, super-stud lady-killer—how could she not reminisce about their very first meeting? After all, it had literally changed her—her self-confidence, the way she viewed herself.

For her part, Harmony was convinced that Pike's being Charlie's best friend and best man was true, divine intervention. Once Ambria and Harmony had dropped Kayla home after the wedding party dinner the night before, they headed right back to the apartment they'd been sharing for over a year, where Harmony lovingly demanded to know why Ambria had never revealed the name of the gorgeous, beefcaked, super-stud lady-killer Madison had brought to supper that special night years before.

"If I'd known his name, I coulda made sure y'all came together again a whole lot sooner than this!" Harmony had exclaimed.

But Ambria explained, as she had four years earlier, that her experience in meeting Pike, and the ensuing life-changing pep talk he'd given her, was something she felt driven to protect—and keeping his name a secret was one way she had determined to do so.

"I always felt like if…if I ever told anyone his name, or showed them the picture hidin' in my wallet, that…well, that somehow it would be tainted, you know?" Ambria confessed to Harmony.

"You've had a picture of him in your wallet all this time?" Harmony gasped. "Good gravy, Ambria Blanchard! You are certainly the best secret-keeper I've ever heard tell of!"

Ambria had shown Harmony the photo of Pike she'd printed the night they'd first met, and Harmony simply shook her head in awe of her friend's ability to keep a secret so well.

"I do understand," Harmony admitted. "And I suppose…well, maybe the time had to be just right for you two to meet again. I mean, maybe if I had known his name and forced a meetin' between the two of you before now…" Harmony shrugged. "As I've always said, divine intervention is at no earthly person's biddin'. It's on heaven's schedule, not ours."

Still, with all Harmony's talk of "divine intervention," Ambria realized Harmony was thinking way beyond reason—diving headfirst into downright fantasy.

"Harm," she began, "don't you go puttin' the horse before the cart, as you always do. Pike and I…we've just run into one another again. It's not like…it's not like we'll end up…romantically entwined or somethin'."

Harmony had laughed, "Oh, ye of little faith, Ambria Blanchard! Things like this don't just happen. There is no such thing as coincidence; you know that. Especially not in matters like this. You two were meant to meet again, when the time was right…and this is the time!"

Nevertheless, no amount of Harmony's insisting that divine intervention was what brought Pike and Ambria together again served to settle Ambria where the matter was concerned. In her mind, it just couldn't be more than happenstance. Oh sure, her heart would leap every time she thought that maybe Harmony was right—that maybe she and Pike would end up in a romantic entwining, or even married. But reality's boot was always there to kick her in the head and knock some sense back into her.

And yet as Ambria sat at the weekly family supper with her daddy and mama and sisters, she couldn't help but hope—hope that maybe Harmony was right, that just maybe there was more to the fact that she and Pike would be thrown together all week because of Harmony and Charlie's wedding. Maybe it wasn't just freakish coincidence. Maybe something marvelous would come of it.

"How's your little summer job goin', Had?" Ambria heard Madison inquire of Hadley. It drew her attention back to the moment at hand.

"Yeah, do you like workin' at the tearoom?" Ambria asked.

Hadley nodded. "Mm-hmm, I do," she answered. "I love servin' the little girls in the children's nooks," she expounded. "They're so cute. I remember when I went with Mama the first time when I was ten and how much I loved it. And to watch the little girls' faces when I bring in their tiered server all piled with sweets and savories and breads—their eyes just sparkle with anticipation. I'm glad I work with the kids' tea parties instead of the adults." Hadley shrugged, smiled, and laughed, "I suppose I just relate better to them."

"Well, I'm certainly glad you're enjoyin' it, Had," Ambria said. "I thought you would. After all, I loved workin' there in the summers when I was in high school."

"Yeah, I do like it," Hadley reiterated. "And you were right, Ambria."

"About what?" Ambria asked.

Hadley giggled. "About the fact that the kids don't like the traditional cucumber sandwiches…any of the little sandwiches that have cucumber! They hardly ever eat them. Most of the time, they're the only thing left on the servers."

Ambria laughed, nodding her head in understanding. "It's funny, isn't it? Miss Jane insists on servin' the cucumber sandwiches no matter what. She's just certain that, someday, every child that attends a tea at Miss Woodhouse's Tearoom will eventually come to love them." She shook her head, still amused. "Three tiers of yummy high-tea treats, and the children almost always leave the cucumber sandwiches as the only thing untouched."

"I am glad you're enjoyin' workin' at the tearoom with Ambria, Had," Madison said. "But I am hopin' you'll work for me one summer. You really do have a natural way with floral arrangin', you know."

Hadley nodded. "Yeah, I still want to do that, Maddy. Maybe next summer," she mused. "I do love your shop. For one thing, it smells divine, and for another, it's so pretty inside."

Ambria looked across the table to Madison—studied her a moment to make certain Madison wasn't miffed that Hadley had chosen to work at the tearoom when the owner, Miss Jane, offered, instead of for Madison at the flower shop. Although Madison had "matured," as her father and mother claimed, she could still be a pill when she had a mind to or when things didn't go exactly as she preferred. But she seemed perfectly happy with Hadley's choice to spend the summer working at the tearoom. Therefore, Ambria exhaled a soft sigh of relief.

"How are the flowers for Harmony's weddin' comin' along, Maddy?" Erica Blanchard asked her oldest daughter. "I know you were worried about the gardenias and peonies for everything...especially for Harmony's bouquet."

"I'm still worried about them," Madison admitted. "But the supplier has assured me they'll be here the night before and that they'll be fresh, fresh, fresh." She shrugged. "So I'm just countin' on it. I'm havin' some backups delivered a couple of days before the weddin', just in case. But I don't want any wilt or discolored edges at all! So I'm hopin' it all goes well."

"Oh, I'm sure it'll all come off just fine," her father assured her.

Madison nodded, took a bite of her meatloaf, and then said, "I just hope Charlie and his groomsmen can handle the gardenia boutonnieres. I don't know very many men who enjoy their strong fragrance...no matter how dreamy it is."

"Has Charlie named his groomsmen yet, Ambria?" Erica asked.

"Oh my, yes!" Madison joined. "The weddin's in a week! Surely he's chosen them by now."

Instantly Ambria felt her blood pressure spike. She knew the moment would eventually arrive when Madison would learn just who was Charlie's best man was. Still, she wished there was some way she could avoid telling her older sister. Ambria wanted to keep the fact that Pike O'Leary would be her escort—that he would be lingering in her life for the next week—a secret. For she was afraid that once Madison discovered the gorgeous, beefcaked, super-stud lady-killer who had slipped through her fingers four years before—well, Ambria was terrified that Madison would try to lasso him back to her. Furthermore, being that Madison was much kinder and much more level-headed than she had been when Pike had come to supper that night—the truth was, Ambria was terrified that Madison actually might manage to rope him.

However, there was no use in putting off the inevitable.

"Yes," Ambria ventured. "Charlie has chosen his groomsmen at last. We all had dinner together at Mancini's last night to get acquainted."

"Well, hallelujah!" Madison exclaimed. "I know that, as patient and understanding as she has been with Charlie's indecision, Harmony was about ready to pull her hair out!"

"Do you know any of the groomsmen, Ambria?" her mother inquired. "How about Charlie's best man? Do you know him?"

Ambria nodded even as her stomach began to churn with anxiety. "I do know a few of them," she proceeded. "Charlie's two brothers and…and I had met his best man once before."

"Oh, really?" Hadley asked. "Where?"

Swallowing the gargantuan lump of anxiety that had formed in her throat, Ambria just said it. "Here, actually. A few years back…when Madison brought him to supper one night."

Everyone at the table stopped chewing—gulping down whatever bite of meatloaf, mashed potatoes, or green beans they'd been working on.

"Who?" Ambria's father asked. "I mean, Madison used to bring men home…guys home…friends home to supper pretty regularly back then."

Ambria looked to Madison. Her eyes were wide with a sort of curious understanding—as if she already knew to whom Ambria was referring but was hoping she might be wrong.

"Pike O'Leary," Madison stated flatly. "Are you tellin' me that Pike O'Leary is Charlie's best man?"

"Yep," was all Ambria could muster as a response.

"Oh, I remember him!" Hadley exclaimed with sudden excitement. "He was freakin' gorgeous!" She looked to her mother, adding, "Remember, Mama? We talked about it after he left…about how gorgeous he was?"

"I remember," Erica admitted as Steve quirked one eyebrow, grinning at his wife with amusement.

"And you're Harmony's maid of honor, Ambria!" Hadley continued to jabber. "So you get to be his counterpart at all the weddin' stuff, right?"

"Yep," Ambria managed again.

"It sure is a small world at times," Steve remarked.

"It sure is," Madison concurred, still staring at Ambria—her eyes still wide with what Ambria hoped was surprise and not envy or resentment.

"He was such a well-mannered and kind young man," Erica sighed with remembered admiration.

"As opposed to my bad-mannered and cruel self back then," Madison mumbled, looking down to her plate.

Ambria felt the discomfort settle over the supper table like a heavy fog. No one knew what to say, because Madison had been a real pill the night she'd brought Pike O'Leary to supper four years ago—and no one was going to deny it. No one was going to confirm it either, but no one was going to deny it.

"Well, I'm as jealous as the day is long, and I'm not afraid to say it," Hadley offered. "That man was gorgeous! Even back then I knew it…and I was only eleven." Hadley looked at Ambria. "Ooo, you'll probably get to dance with him and be photographed with him. Yummy!"

"Yep," Ambria agreed as her heart leapt from the pit of her stomach back into her chest at the thought of Hadley's suggestions becoming a reality.

"You can say more than 'yep,' Ambria," Madison said, smiling then. "That was four years ago, and I'm completely over it...over him, anyway. He wasn't my type, and I certainly wasn't his type, so I say, have fun this week! At least you'll have the company of a handsome man here and there while you're gettin' through all this weddin' stuff. I'm only doin' the flowers, and I'm stressed out. I can't imagine what this comin' week will be like for all of you."

"Yeah, Ambria," Hadley added, winking at her. "It might be crazy, but at least it'll be fun. And maybe you'll even find yourself makin' out with that handsome best man a time or two."

"Hadley," Erica kindly scolded, "Ambria is not goin' to be makin' out with some man she hardly knows."

"Why not?" Hadley brazenly inquired. "If I had the chance to make out with Pike O'Leary, I wouldn't miss it for the world."

"Steven!" Erica exclaimed with worry as she looked to her husband for support.

Ambria exchanged knowing glances with Madison. Oh, their little sister had developed a sense of tact, at last—but with it came an almost insatiable desire to keep their mother in a perpetual state of shock and awe.

"Well," their father began, "the way I remember it, that Pike O'Leary was a good-lookin' dude. I suppose any girl would leap at the chance to make out with him. So I'm with Hadley." He looked to Ambria, pointed his fork at her, and said, "If the opportunity arises for you and Pike to get a little jiggy with it...well, I'd make out with him if I were you."

"Steven!" Erica nearly shrieked. "What on earth are you doin'? Encouragin' our daughters to…to…to…"

"Hadley's just messin' with you, Mama," Madison giggled. "As usual."

"No, I'm not. Not this time," Hadley assured everyone. She looked to Ambria and added, "If I were in your shoes this week, Ambria, I'd be sure I found a way to draw Pike into my arms usin' my feminine wiles."

"Hadley!" Erica gasped.

"Okay, okay," Steve chuckled as everyone—with the exception of Erica—burst into laughter. "That's enough teasin' for one night. We're goin' to give your mama a heart attack here pretty soon if we don't quit it."

As the laughter settled, Hadley reached over, placing a comforting hand on her mother's arm. "I'm sorry, Mama," she apologized. "I just couldn't resist."

Erica exhaled a heavy sigh, nodded, and said, "You're goin' to be the death of me, Hadley. I swear!"

Yet as everyone returned their attention to supper, Hadley leaned over to Ambria, whispering, "But if I were you, I sure wouldn't miss the chance to make out with that hot piece of beefcake this week."

Ambria giggled. Hadley was so hilarious, always so enjoyable to be around. In that moment, Ambria wished she still lived at home so that she could appreciate and savor her little sister more often.

♥

As Ambria strolled down the sidewalk in front of the apartment complex, she thought how much more pleasant the weekly supper at her daddy and mama's house had been once she realized Madison wasn't going to go ballistic concerning Pike O'Leary's being

Charlie's best man (and thereby Ambria's counterpart) for the wedding. Ambria had known her anxiety over the inevitability of Madison's finding out about Pike was weighing heavy on her before supper. But she hadn't realized just how weighty it was until the fact had been revealed and Madison had not freaked out. In truth, Ambria had thoroughly enjoyed the time with her family—even Madison. After supper, Ambria had taken Chunk for his walk and then sat under the big willow tree on the front lawn with him for a while. And although she'd enjoyed ending the evening spending time with her beloved family pet, it did make her rather weepy and sad to see Chunk aging so quickly. Her father had brought Chunk home to the family when Ambria was only ten years old. She couldn't imagine home and life without him, and the fact he was showing his age made her heart feel sore.

As she unlocked the front door to her apartment, Ambria's thoughts were still lingering on sweet, cherished, elderly Chunk. Thus, when she stepped inside to see Harmony and Charlie sitting on the sofa in the front room—and Pike sitting on the love seat—she was a little rattled.

"Oh…hi," Ambria stammered as she closed the apartment door behind her and dropped her purse to one side of it.

"Charlie and Pike are here," Harmony chirped, explaining the obvious. "They stopped by to help me with the schedule for next week."

"Great!" Ambria exclaimed. Her melancholy over Chunk evaporated quickly as one look at Pike caused goose bumps to ripple over her arms and butterfly wings began to beat against each other in her stomach. *He's surreal!* she thought to herself as she permitted herself to stare at Pike for a moment. And he was! It seemed that every time she saw Pike O'Leary, he somehow appeared even better looking than he had the time before.

"So are we goin' to be runnin' errands every day and partyin' like it's 1999 every night?" Ambria asked.

"For the most part," Charlie answered.

Ambria noted how tired he looked—how overwhelmed.

"Oh, now quit, darlin'," Harmony giggled, slapping Charlie playfully on the thigh. "You know I won't make you run all the errands."

"Have a seat, Ambria," Pike said then, patting the empty seat next to him on the love seat. "You don't wanna miss out on all this fun, now do you?"

Just the sound of her name crossing Pike's lips—the sound of his voice pronouncing it—made Ambria's knees feel weak.

"Of course not," Ambria said, forcing herself to have the confidence to stride to the love seat and sit down next to Pike. "I don't want anything to slip through the cracks. Isn't that right, Harm?"

"Exactly," Harmony confirmed.

Ambria giggled a little when she heard quiet groans escape both Charlie's and Pike's throats. Every woman everywhere knew that all the buttons and bows of a wedding were pure torture for men. It was why Harmony had been so patient and understanding with Charlie—giving him as little foo-foo responsibility as possible. And for his part, Charlie had been very patient and supportive. Still, Ambria could see it was wearing on him. Most likely Charlie just wanted the wedding to be over so he and Harmony could get on with their lives together.

"So let's go down the list," Harmony began. Exhaling a heavy sigh, indicating that even she was tired of the foo-foo, Harmony continued, "We've got the bachelor-slash-bachelorette party on Thursday night nailed down. Accordin' to Madison, the flowers are on schedule. Caterin' is fine, setup and decoratin' is fine. We girls have one more meetin' about our presentation to Charlie and his groomsmen on Wednesday mornin'. Dresses, check. Charlie and the boys have shirts, matchin' ties, dress pants, and shoes all lined out."

"I'm so glad you're not makin' them tuxedo it out, Harm," Ambria offered. "Accordin' to the forecast, it's really goin' to be muggy this next week."

"Oh, me too," Harmony agreed. She leaned over, placing a loving kiss on Charlie's cheek. "That was Charlie's idea. And a great one!"

"I do like that the two of you are havin' one big party for your friends, instead of doin' the bachelor and bachelorette party thing," Pike commented. "For one thing, it's classy."

"Thanks, Pike," Harmony said, smiling.

"And for another thing, it alleviates Ambria and me of havin' to throw separate parties," Pike chuckled.

Charlie and Harmony smiled too. "And there is that," Harmony agreed. Having suddenly remembered something, she continued, "Oh! I wanted to ask you about somethin', Charlie. Who did you say you ordered the groom's cake from?"

"Betty Lou's Bakery—that local place here in Mt. Pleasant," Charlie answered. "Mom said they're great."

"Oh, they are!" Harmony exclaimed. "You're so smart, sugar." She leaned over and kissed him on the mouth. "What did you order? Somethin' outrageous? Or somethin' plain and simple?"

"Somethin' plain and simple," Charlie mumbled, returning her kiss. "My cake will be decorated to look like a giant Oreo cookie."

"Oh, I love that!" Harmony laughed, kissing Charlie again. "You love Oreos so much! It's perfect. You're so clever, honey!"

"I'm glad you approve, muffin," Charlie said as he gathered Harmony in his arms and began to kiss her like he would never get enough of her kiss.

Ambria giggled as she and Pike looked at each other—each amused by the soon-to-be-newlyweds' affections.

"So," Pike began, "looks like we're goin' to have a few moments alone here." His smile broadened, and he winked at Ambria. "So since Harmony's movin' out, are you lookin' for a new roommate?"

Ambria shrugged. "I don't know yet," she admitted. "Truly, I can't imagine livin' with anybody else. Harmony and I have been so close for forever—since we were little girls—and she's been my only roommate." She shook her head. "Still, it is a two-bedroom apartment, and I don't know if I want to handle the rent on my own, you know?"

"Well, here's an idea. I'm lookin' for a place just like this. I could move in next week if you're willin'," Pike suggested.

Ambria felt her eyebrows arch in astonishment. He couldn't possibly be serious. And yet she saw no expression of mischief on his face—just that of deadpan sincerity.

"I thought you owned a house outside of Charleston," Harmony inquired, having looked up from her shared affections with Charlie.

"Hush, woman!" Pike teased then. "I'm workin' on seducin' your maid of honor here. You go on about your own business."

Even though she was relieved to know Pike had been kidding about wanting to be her roommate, Ambria blushed at what he'd said to Harmony—that he was working on seducing her. Oh sure, she knew he was kidding about that, as well—but it still thrilled her through and through.

"Now, where were we?" Pike said, returning his attention to Ambria. "Ah yes…you're indecisive about a new roommate, and now you know I already own a house and that I was just flirtin' with you. So…let's move on, shall we?"

"Sure," Ambria giggled—delighted that he had indeed been flirting with her.

"Well, I've had a question I have wanted to ask you since I first saw you that night at supper at your folks' house," he said.

"And what's that?" Ambria ventured. Even though her heart rate had increased with trepidation at wondering what on earth he could've wanted to ask her back then, she was courageous and nodded with encouragement.

"I've always wondered," Pike began. Ambria smiled as he reached into his shirt pocket and produced two cinnamon toothpicks. He handed one to her and popped the other in his mouth. "How come your parents didn't name you Cinnamon?"

Ambria laughed, "What? Why in the world would they have named me Cinnamon?"

She placed the cinnamon toothpick on her tongue, enjoying the spicy tingle—and she wondered if kissing Pike O'Leary would tingle just as much.

"Because of your hair," he answered. "Cinnamon is my favorite flavor, and when I first set eyes on you that night, I remember thinkin', *Wow! That girl's hair is so perfect…like the perfect cinnamon color. I wonder why her folks didn't just name her Cinnamon?* I really did think that," he explained.

Ambria laughed, entirely amused and utterly flattered. "You did not," she playfully accused.

"I did too!" Pike assured her. "Later on that night when we were standin' outside of your house talkin', I remember thinkin' that I wanted to reach out and lick your head—you know, to see if your hair really did taste like cinnamon."

"You did not!" Ambria giggled, delighted by his flirtation.

"I did too!" Pike reiterated.

"Well, I'm glad you didn't…because you would've been horribly disappointed to find out it tastes like shampoo and conditioner," Ambria laughed, shaking her head.

She gasped, however, as Pike quickly leaned over and actually licked the top of her head.

"It tastes just like cinnamon!" he proclaimed. "I knew it would!"

Ambria shook her head, blushing, giggling, horrified, and yet simultaneously all atingle.

"It does not!" she laughed.

"It does so," he argued. "Here…taste it," he demanded, taking a long strand of her hair and holding it up toward her mouth. "Seriously…taste it."

In an effort to prove that her hair did not taste like cinnamon, Ambria accepted the length of her own hair, placing it in her mouth a moment.

For an instant she was astonished—for she did indeed taste cinnamon. Nevertheless, it only took a nanosecond for her to realize that she had been sucking on a cinnamon toothpick—just as Pike had been.

"Har-har," she said, smiling at him. "It's those cinnamon toothpicks of yours. That's all it is."

And then, Ambria's mouth dropped open in disbelieving wonderment as Pike took the strand of her hair from her hand, drawing it to his mouth, and placing it against his tongue at the same place she had just tasted it.

"Nope…it's cinnamon," he determined. "And not from the toothpick."

"Dude!" Charlie exclaimed then, arresting Ambria's attention as well as Pike's.

Ambria looked over to the sofa to see both Charlie and Harmony staring at them with puzzled expressions.

"What?" Pike asked.

"Dude, if you want to kiss her, just kiss her," Charlie instructed. "Don't suck on her hair. That's weird, man."

But Pike shrugged, and Ambria watched the toothpick in his mouth move from one side to the other. "It tastes like cinnamon. And anyway, mind your own business, man. You just concentrate on lip-smacking with your pretty mermaid there, all right?"

Charlie chuckled, gathered Harmony back into his arms, and began kissing her again.

For her part, Ambria looked back to Pike, still stunned that he'd licked her hair and then tasted the same strand of it that she had.

"Also," Pike continued, as if nothing at all were out of the ordinary, "that dog y'all had that night…Chunk. Is he named after the kid in the old Goonies movie?"

In truth, Ambria's thought process ground like the gears of a 1965 Ford pickup as she shifted from the fact Pike claimed her hair tasted like cinnamon to where Chunk had gotten his name.

"Um…uh…yeah," she stammered. "We…we named him after Chunk in *The Goonies*."

"Cool," Pike said, nodding. "I wondered."

For twenty minutes—until Harmony and Charlie finally remembered that there were two other people in the room and wedding plans to finalize—Pike and Ambria shared lighthearted, very satisfying, and entertaining conversation. Yet for everything else they talked about—for every like or dislike they revealed to one another—Ambria could not believe Pike had not only flirted with her but also tasted her hair.

Even later that night, as she lay in bed thinking over every moment she'd spent with Pike that evening, her arms prickled with goose bumps and her stomach swirled with enchanted butterflies every time she thought of it.

"He licked my hair," she whispered to herself. Smiling with delight, she verbally reminded herself, "He actually tasted my hair."

CHAPTER FOUR

The next two days were fantastic! Oh, certainly there were errands to run, various and sundry things concerning the wedding and festivities that needed checking on. But being that Harmony's dad had rented the luxurious house for the bridesmaids and groomsmen to spend the week leading up to the wedding, every evening was more like a vacation or party than anything else. And although the constant socializing would normally have worn Ambria to the core, she found that she reveled in it and for one reason: the fact that she spent nearly every waking moment in Pike's company.

Any time Ambria needed to run an errand for Harmony, Pike offered to go with her—even drove. Any time everyone else was off doing different thises and thats, Pike stayed at the house with Ambria, where they'd sit together on one of the sofas in one of the several dens. Oh sure, Harmony, Charlie, and everyone else were hanging out there most of the time, especially in the large entertainment room. There was always someone playing darts, shuffleboard, or cards, or swimming in the enormous pool out back. And sure, Ambria and Pike interacted with their friends—but not for the majority of the time. The majority of each day they spent just the two of them together, in one way or the other. Whether playing games or in the pool or running errands for the wedding, they were together. Ambria's favorite time spent with Pike, however, was definitely in the evenings—just sitting somewhere, talking, laughing, and thoroughly getting to know each other.

In fact, Wednesday morning—during the rehearsal of the dance Harmony and her bridesmaids would be presenting to Charlie at the big party the next evening—Ambria found she was downright impatient. All she could think about was getting the rehearsal over with so that she could get back to the house—so that she could get back to Pike.

Finally, after a couple of hours of practice, Harmony announced, "Well, it's not goin' to get any more perfect than that! Am I right, girls?" Everyone agreed with either a verbal response or an emphatic nod. "Then let's get back to the house and have some fun! Goodness knows we deserve it after all this hard work, right?"

Ambria didn't wait one second. She lit out through the dance studio door, hopped into her car, and even broke the speed limit a little, so desperate was she to get back to Pike. Not only was he the only person she wanted to be with for the rest of the day—*Be with forever*, she thought to herself—she had a deep, persistent worry that he'd somehow lose interest in her if she were away from him too long. Oh, she knew it was irrational—downright stalker mentality almost—but she couldn't help it! Pike O'Leary had her in his grip, and he didn't even know it! She wouldn't tell anyone she was obsessed with him—obsessed by being with him—but she was. He lit such a fire of intrigue, energy, and joy in her heart! Not to mention the fact that he incited a near overwhelming physical attraction in her—a height of desire she'd never experienced before. Yep, she was obsessed, all right. And admittedly a little panicked— for she couldn't help but wonder if he would just disappear from her life again once the wedding was over, drive off into the sunset just as he had four years before.

Ambria smiled and giggled to herself as she pulled in behind Pike's vintage canary-yellow Mustang. She thought of the conversation they'd had about it just the day before—when he explained that he just couldn't "put the ol' girl out to pasture," as he phrased it. After all, he'd had her since he was sixteen. And as old as she was under the hood, she still looked great from the outside. Pike had explained to Ambria that he did indeed own a pickup—one that wasn't nearly as old as the Ford Mustang's sixteen years. He drove his truck eighty percent of the time. But once in a while he took "Bee," as he called the Mustang, out for a day or two, just to let her know how special she was.

As Ambria parked her own car behind Bee, her heart swelled with admiration and a feeling of kindred to Pike over his affection for the car. She became attached to inanimate objects too—especially if they had a nostalgic or emotional history with her. She thought of the little Lefton china dog figurine that sat on the bookshelf in her bedroom. She'd had it ever since she could remember, even though she couldn't remember who had given it to her. Every day she winked at the little dog, sometimes stroking its nose or saying good morning or good night. She knew it wasn't a living thing. But to Ambria it had a life all its own—one that it had shared with her, always.

She laughed out loud when she thought of the story Pike had told her of how his father told him he would eventually have to get rid of the Mustang, citing that a car was too large to be a keepsake. Still, Ambria's smile broadened as she walked past Bee, gently caressing her hood as she started toward the house—because she understood how Pike felt about her. Bee was part of his past, part of his life. Therefore, even though she wasn't a living creature with a soul, she owned a piece of Pike's heart.

Ambria was smiling and thinking how much she'd like to own a piece of Pike's heart when she entered the nine-bedroom, four-bathroom luxury home reserved for the wedding attendants. But her smile vanished when she walked into the entertainment room in search of Pike, to find none other than Madison standing there talking with Pike and Charlie. In truth, Ambria stopped dead in her tracks. She'd seen the familiar expression many times on her big sister's face over the past decade—been witness to the way she flirtatiously tossed her head and ran her fingers through her long blonde hair. These were the mannerisms Madison employed when entrapment was on her mind—and Ambria knew Madison didn't have her eyes set on Charlie as her prey. She was after Pike!

Yet just as Ambria's heart was threatening to plummet to the pit of her stomach—just as all the nasty little whispers of losing her self-confidence began to ricochet around in her brain in telling her that Pike might just decide Madison was prettier, kinder, and more his type than she'd been four years ago—Pike glanced up, catching sight of her.

"Oh, there you are!" he called as he turned and strode toward her. "Where have you been? You've been gone forever."

"We, uh…we were just…" Ambria stammered as Pike reached her, taking hold of her hand.

"Well, your sister has been here for almost forty minutes waitin' on Harmony," he explained, looking exactly as if Ambria had somehow saved him from a fate worse than death. "She has some questions about the flowers or somethin'," he finished. Then, turning so that he stood facing Ambria with his back to Madison and Charlie, the color drained from his handsome face, his eyes widened with apparent anxiety, and he whispered, "Help me! I think she wants me."

As stressed out as the sight of Madison had instantly made her—as worried as she had immediately been about Madison's winning Pike for her own—Pike's humble, shocked expression combined with his plea for assistance was priceless—hilarious even!

"Of course she wants you!" Ambria laughed in a whisper. "We all want you, you dork!"

Did she just imply that she wants me? Pike thought to himself as he studied Ambria's pretty face—her cinnamon-tasting hair and alluring rosy-pink lips. The uneasiness that Madison had ignited in him—by bombarding him with her flirtations the last near hour—vanished.

For the past couple of days, he and Ambria had been nearly inseparable. Not only had it given him cause to think that she really did like him as much as he liked her, but Pike's entire outlook on his future had begun to morph to a dreamlike venue he hadn't conceived it ever would before meeting up with Ambria again. And now she was standing right in front of him, telling him that "we all want you." Of course, he didn't give a rat's ass about any other woman wanting him—but Ambria had said "we," implying she did. And that was an entirely different ballgame—a game changer—the opening he'd been hoping and waiting for.

"And she'll be relentless until she gets what she wants," Ambria whispered, her smile fading, her amber-brown eyes looking suddenly moist and sad.

Pike's eyes narrowed as he studied Ambria differently then. Her laughter had indeed been contrived, her smile forced. It appeared that Madison could still pull the rug of self-confidence out from under her little sister's feet when she wanted to.

"Well, then she's in for a hell of a disappointment if I'm her target," he grumbled. "Because I could put your sister under the table when it comes to bein' relentless about what I want." He leaned down, placing a soft, lingering kiss on her cheek and whispering, "And I want you."

Ambria held her breath, uncertain she had heard Pike correctly.

But then he added, "So let her put that in her pipe and smoke it, baby," before winking at her and sauntering toward the entertainment room. He looked back at her, adding, "Meet you on the sofa in a few minutes, okay?"

"O-okay," Ambria managed to respond.

Ambria heard the front door open and turned to see Harmony step into the house. "My stars, Ambria!" Harmony exclaimed. "You were off like a bat out of hellfire and brimstone, girl! Is everything okay?"

"Oh yes," Ambria assured her friend. "I just wanted to get showered and changed and things."

"And back to cuddlin' up with Pike, no doubt," Harmony whispered as she neared. "I don't blame you."

Ambria blushed. Oh sure, Harmony knew Ambria was dead gone on Pike. She not only understood but encouraged it, as well. And Ambria figured it was why Harmony's smile faded and she drew in a breath of irritation when she looked up and saw Madison coming toward them.

"I see your sister is here for no apparent good reason," Harmony mumbled, "though I can guess what her reason is."

"Somethin' about the flowers, I think," Ambria offered.

"Mm-hmm," Harmony grumbled. "She's got flowers on her mind as much as she does my fine white fanny. And here she comes."

"Hi, baby sister," Madison greeted with a hug as she stepped up to where Harmony and Ambria stood. "Are you havin' a fun week?"

"Yes, ma'am," Ambria answered with a smile. She was still trying to give Madison the benefit of the doubt. Maybe she really did just have some things about the flowers to go over with Harmony.

"Oh good," Madison giggled. Turning her attention to Harmony, she began, "I just wanted to go over a few last-minute things with you about all the flowers, Harmony. They are so delicate in nature that I wanted to be certain I've got everything just the way you want it."

"Okay, Madison," Harmony said. "Let me just go change, and I'll be right back. Okay?"

"You bet," Madison agreed.

Harmony glanced to Ambria, adding a silent nod of reassurance just before she hurried off.

"I better get changed too," Ambria suggested. "I probably smell like a wet puppy." She forced a smile to her older sister. "I'll see you later, Maddy. And thanks for doin' Harmony's flowers. She's so excited about them."

Madison smiled with pride. "They're goin' to be gorgeous, just gorgeous!"

"Oh, good!" Ambria exclaimed. "Well, I'll see you later."

But as she turned to leave, it happened.

"And to think…I used to tease you about your big boobs bein' a bad thing," Madison laughed quietly.

"What?" Ambria asked. She was stunned that Madison would drop back four years into her mean-girl self.

"Your boobs," Madison said. "It's obvious Pike is interested in you. Charlie says the two of you are nearly inseparable. And you don't think he's attracted to your sparklin', outgoin' personality, do you?"

"You're so nasty, Madison," Ambria scolded. She was angry—angry and hurt. Madison was her sister, after all. Shouldn't she expect more kindness? Especially now that they were grown up?

"Oh, don't get your panties in a wad, baby sister," Madison giggled. "I see he's got his eye on you now, so I'll back off and let you have him. But seriously, Ambria…way to rock those freaky big yabahos of yours. I guess we both know what makes all the difference in a woman for Pike O'Leary, now don't we?"

"I guess we do, Maddy," Ambria said through clenched teeth. "But here's a little advice: jealousy, that ol' green envy…well, it is not your best color."

Without another word, Ambria turned and headed toward the bedroom she was sharing with Harmony.

Choking back tears of hurt and anger—of mammoth frustration—she closed the door to the bedroom behind her and began to strip out of her rehearsal clothes. Harmony was already in the shower, and Ambria was grateful. With any luck, she could slip into the shower just after Harmony was finished and avoid letting Harmony see how upset she was.

"You okay?" Harmony called from the shower.

"Yeah. Just feelin' grimy after practicin'," Ambria fibbed.

"Well, I'm almost finished, and then I can get out there and see what Madison wants and then send her on her way," Harmony explained. "She didn't upset you, did she?"

"Not any more than usual," Ambria fibbed again.

"Well, good!" Harmony stated. "I wouldn't want to have to wring her scrawny little neck before I get my flowers."

"Yeah," Ambria called, still battling to keep from bursting into tears.

For no matter what her common sense was telling her— reminding her that Madison was just jealous—Madison's words and implications had stung. Furthermore, they had planted deep seeds of doubt—doubt that Ambria's personality was really what was attracting Pike to her. After all, he had made it quite clear that he liked her—had boldly said he'd wanted her right there in the entryway just minutes before. Yet, that old dirty devil doubt had been planted deep in Ambria's mind years and years before, and although she'd beat him down over the years, he was making himself known with a vengeance in those moments.

"Okay, I'm out if you want to hop in," Harmony called.

"Thanks," Ambria said, heading into the bathroom.

"Here's my shower cap if you don't want to wash your hair," Harmony said. Having finished wrapping herself in a towel, she pulled the shower cap off her head, allowing her long, beautiful dark hair to cascade over her shoulders.

"Thanks," Ambria said, accepting the shower cap. "I'll wait 'til tonight to wash it. I might skip the dinner and dancin' tonight, Harm. I'm worn out today for some reason. Some soakin' in the pool all by myself sounds good. You won't mind if I stay here and swim tonight, do you?"

Harmony turned to face the mirror, watching as Ambria tucked her gorgeous auburn hair up into the shower cap.

"Not at all, darlin'," she said, looking back to her own reflection so that Ambria could finish undressing and get into the shower. "I've got to admit, I've been amazed at how much socializin' you've been up to so far. I figured you would've wanted some downtime long before now. Then again…Pike does seem to fill your cup, so to speak, more than anyone I've ever seen with you before."

"He does do that," Ambria admitted.

Harmony frowned as she looked into the mirror. She knew darn well that Madison had said something to upset her BFF. But she also knew that Ambria wasn't about to let anything dampen any part of the week leading up to the wedding—especially her own emotions or fatigue. So she didn't press her friend, determined to keep the conversation lighthearted.

"Do you think Charlie will like our performance?" she asked Ambria instead.

"Are you kiddin'?" Ambria giggled. "The man goes bananas when you're simply wearin' your hard shoes! He'll go bonkers when he sees it!"

Harmony already knew Charlie would love the Irish step dance performance she and the girls had been working on for him. It would be a party he'd never forget, that was for certain. Still, she knew it was important to make small talk when Ambria was working through whatever negative emotions Madison had poured out over her and caused her to be enduring.

"Oh, I hope he really does like it," Harmony said, raking her fingers through her hair. "I think tomorrow night will be so much fun! You're smart to take tonight off from all the ho-ha, Am. That way you'll be ready for the big event tomorrow night."

"That's a good point, Harm," Ambria agreed.

It was time to leave her friend to her own thoughts then. Harmony knew Ambria well, and she knew she needed some quiet moments to recover from her meeting with Madison.

"Well, I'm goin' to throw somethin' on and head back," she said. "Take your time, and don't worry about not comin' with us all tonight. I know you'll enjoy the time alone…and you deserve it! I've about wrung you out like a worn dishcloth these past weeks."

"No, you have not," Ambria giggled—which Harmony knew was a fib. "But I will enjoy the pool by myself a lot more than I enjoy it in the group, you know that."

"Oh, I know that, girl," Harmony laughed. Harmony looked at herself one last time in the mirror—winked at her sly reflection as an idea began to form in her sneaky little mind. "I do know that," she whispered to herself as she left the bathroom.

Hurriedly Harmony pulled on some comfortable clothes. She wanted to get out of the bedroom and to Pike before Ambria had a chance to finish showering and dress.

Oh, Harmony was more than happy for Ambria to take a break from all the socializing by staying at the house that night. But she wouldn't be alone—no indeed! Harmony would just drop a little bug in Pike's ear—and she knew that Charlie's best friend would be over the moon to know he would have the chance to be alone with Ambria that night. With no prying eyes—no overwhelming social network around to intrude—Harmony figured that her BFF and Charlie's BFF would finally have the chance to really get to know each other.

"Yep," Harmony whispered to herself as she dashed out of the bedroom in search of Pike. "I'm goin' to make sure you really enjoy your night off, Ambria Blanchard. Mm-hmmm!"

CHAPTER FIVE

"Ahhhhh," Ambria sighed. The house was so quiet. It was heavenly!

As she stepped out onto the back patio and started toward the pool, she remembered Harmony's paranoid, yet wise, worrisome warning.

"I don't know how I feel about you goin' swimmin' when no one else is here, Am," Harmony had worried aloud. "I mean…it's not really very safe."

Ambria had been touched by Harmony's concern. Yet she had assured Harmony she only meant to sit on the underwater, graduated steps leading down into the four-foot end of the pool and relax—not actually swim. And Harmony's countenance had brightened as her concern lessened.

And now, as Ambria tossed her long pink sarong onto one of the patio chairs and stepped down onto the first step leading into the pool, she smiled. This was just what she needed: time without everyone else around so that she could process what had happened with Madison earlier in the day. She'd already worked through it for the most part, knowing that Madison was just jealous because the man who had slipped through her fingers four years ago was now paying attention to her little sister. Still, Madison's hurtful comments resurrected the self-image issues Ambria had grappled with since the day puberty had begun its cruel appearance on her body in the fifth grade.

The truth was, she still hated her boobs! For years she'd even struggled with resenting the male gender because they were so physically motivated. Having endured the teasing and taunting that erupts in children for some devilish reason, all through sixth grade and then into seventh and eighth—having tried to ignore the whistles, catcalls, and lewd innuendos heaved, flung, and pitched at her for the last eleven years—having been groped by boys she thought were decent—having been asked on dates and to school dances just so boys could try to cop a feel—it had all built up such a resentment toward her own body and men in general. Ambria had worked very hard the past four years to overcome her negative emotions about her own body, as well as her resentment of men and their "urges."

After that night—the night Pike O'Leary had given her the pep talk of all pep talks, even telling her that her boobs were perfect—Ambria had realized that there was nothing wrong with her. There wasn't even anything wrong with her having a great figure. She'd begun to be conscious of the fact that it wasn't every boy or man who looked at her chest instead of her eyes when he was talking to her. It wasn't every boy or man who tried to "accidentally" brush up against her chest when she was attending parties and dances. It was only the jerks. Furthermore, it was only people like Madison— envious women—who made fun of her Raquel Welch, classic- hourglass body shape. In fact, what was deemed an attractive figure had changed so much over the last sixty years, most people didn't even know what an hourglass figure was, let alone knowing what one looked like in real life. Skinny, skinny, ultra skinny was what was considered attractive sometimes, while big booties and thick waists were what everyone deemed sexy at other times. It was a lose-lose situation for most women, and Ambria had learned how to be glad that she was shaped the way she was shaped. Even if she did still have to endure the occasional disgusting proposition in line at the grocery store.

Madison was jealous of Ambria's figure. What Pike had said that night four years before was true. And obviously, not much had changed in that regard.

Therefore, as Ambria sighed while sitting down on the second step down into the pool, allowing the water to lap over her legs and waist, she knew that what she was really struggling to swallow was the fact that Madison had been so merciless and cruel to her that day.

"What a turd," Ambria mumbled aloud. In that moment, she wished—as she had many times before—that some poor sucker would come along and marry Madison and whisk her away to life in California, or any other state on the other side of the country. The fact was, Madison wore Ambria out.

"Mind if I join you?"

Ambria gasped, startled by the sound of Pike's voice.

"Wh-what are you doin' here?" she asked as she stared up at the gorgeous, beefcaked, super-stud lady-killer standing there smiling down at her. "I-I thought everyone was at supper."

"Everyone is," he answered. "Except for me and you."

Without waiting for her response as to whether she minded if he joined her—which of course she did not—Pike slipped off his pool sandals and stepped down onto the first step in the pool.

"Oh good," he said. "I was afraid it would be too warm, you know?"

"Nope, it's just right. Nice and cool, but not cold," Ambria commented as she stared at him. He was wearing blue board shorts and a white T-shirt.

Ambria scooched down another step so that the pool water covered her shoulders. For all her determination to be confident, she had suddenly realized she was wearing the blue sequined bathing suit with side cutouts that Harmony had gifted her. Oh sure, she'd gone swimming in the pool since the group arrived at the rental house, but she'd worn her more conservative long tankini top with matching shorts. In the stupid suit Harmony had given her, she suddenly felt very vulnerable—as well as half naked.

"Uh oh," Pike laughed, smiling down at her. "You're already tryin' to run away from me, are you?"

"N-no," Ambria fibbed. "I was just…adjustin' to the water slowly, and—"

"Liar," Pike chuckled.

Ambria's gaze was utterly transfixed then as Pike reached over his right shoulder with his right hand, stripping the white T-shirt off over his head and tossing it to land in a heap next to Ambria's sarong on the patio chair.

Oh, it wasn't that she hadn't seen the man bare-chested before. After all, Pike had gone swimming with everyone else on two occasions since first bunking at the house. But this was different! First of all, afraid of being found out—of everyone else being able to read her expressions whenever she looked at Pike—Ambria had been very focused on either not looking at Pike directly when he was in the pool or making sure she looked only at his face. She'd certainly seen the other bridesmaids checking Pike out in the pool, and their awed expressions were enough to verify to her that he was ripped when stripped. But for her part, she'd avoided studying his physique when he'd been wearing only board shorts before.

Now, however, it was a different story. Pike O'Leary was up close and personal and stepping into the pool! Moreover, he was looking like the great Greek titan Atlas, chiseled out of warm, bronzed granite as he did so. His overall musculature—his broad chest and shoulders and his cliché washboard stomach—was nothing short of perfect. If Aphrodite and Adonis had had a long-lost son, Pike O'Leary was him.

Superb. Massively superb, Ambria thought as Pike sat down on the step next to her.

"Ahhh," Pike sighed. "Listen to that quiet. Nothin' but water lappin' in the pool, crickets close by, and a little bitty breeze stirrin' the leaves. Fine, fine, very fine."

Ambria smiled, pleased by his musing.

"Harmony made you stay behind, didn't she?" she playfully accused. "She was afraid I'd drown if someone wasn't here with me, wasn't she?"

Pike grinned at her. "Nope. Well, she did tell me you were wrung out from bein' around people for days on end." He shrugged his broad, broad, bronzed shoulders. "And quite frankly, so am I." He looked at her, his grin expanding into a smile. "But she didn't tell me you were stayin' behind so I could be your lifeguard, sugar. She told me because she knew I would jump at the chance to get you alone all to myself."

Even though Ambria's heart fluttered with delight, she had to play coy. After all, it was the southern belle thing to do.

"Oh, that's why she told you, hmm?" she asked, feigning doubt.

"Yes, indeed," Pike assured her.

"Hmm," Ambria hummed with skepticism.

"You know that you do have the perfect mermaid hair," Pike said. He reached out, tugging a little on Ambria's ponytail. She'd pulled her hair up to keep it from getting too wet, being that she had planned on just sitting in the pool and not swimming.

"Oh, do I?" she flirted. Silently Ambria admitted to herself that she already felt better. Just Pike's company was like some sort of healing salve to her mind, her emotions, her mood.

"Is that why Harmony is dressin' y'all up like mermaids for her weddin'?" he teased, grinning at her as he continued to play with her ponytail. "Did your cinnamon mermaid hair inspire it all? I swear, me and Charlie were afraid she'd be havin' the groomsmen wearin' mermen tails and whatnot. Charlie says it was mermaid this and mermaid that right from the beginnin'." He paused, moving closer to her—until the side of his muscular arm was flush against her arm.

"No. It wasn't me and my hair," Ambria giggled, flattered. "Harmony has loved mermaids...well, for as long as I can remember. I think she always wanted some sort of tribute to them in her weddin' one day. And so, here we are...with sequins comin' out of our ears and y'all groomsmen wearin' dark blue suits, green shirts, and all."

"I'm told they're asparagus-colored shirts," Pike interjected, "although me and Charlie get to wear pink shirts, from what I understand."

Ambria giggled. "Yes, you do. Charlie, because he's the queen mermaid's groom and seashell pink is Harmony's favorite color. And you, because I get to be the mermaid in pink...as her maid of honor and all. And you and I need to match."

Pike winked at her. His eyes narrowed with such an alluring quality that the butterflies living in Ambria's stomach erupted into a mushroom cloud of fluttering wings and excitement.

"I think you and I already match," he said in a low, titillatingly provocative voice. "With or without our coordinatin' mermaid and merman attire. Don't you?"

"Oh now…what are you up to, Mr. O'Leary, that you're slatherin' me with flirtation out here in the pool?" Ambria asked, smiling at him—entirely mesmerized by the smoldering quality in his blue, blue, bluest eyes.

"I like you," he stated. "I figure you should know that by now. Still, it's always best to be sure you know it. So I'm tellin' you."

Ambria's heart leapt in her bosom as warmth enveloped her. "Well, I like you too," she somehow found the courage to confess.

His grin lengthened. "However, there is one revelation I have to make right here and right now…before we slip any deeper into this pool tonight."

Ambria struggled to keep the smile on her face as trepidation rose in her. What would he reveal to her? She was suddenly a nervous wreck.

"Oh dear," she began, somehow able to keep the countenance of playfulness and flirtation in her expression. "And what might that be?"

Pike's own grinned lessened a bit. "Well, I'll just spit it out, and we'll clean it up later. So here goes." Looking straight into her eyes—the blue of his seeming to pierce the soft brown of her own—he said, "Well, Miss Blanchard…I don't like your sister Madison. And you want to know why?"

Even as her heart leapt from anxiety back to elation at his announcement, she tried to appear calm. In truth, she wanted to throw her arms around his neck and kiss him hard on the mouth—on his sexy, perfect mouth—in appreciation of his not liking Madison.

"And why is that?" she inquired as her heart began pounding in her chest—pounding with happiness, pounding with attraction and desire.

"Because she's a pretentious phony," he answered. "I...I don't want to make you mad at me, but I could tell today—after you changed and came in to sit with me on the sofa—Madison upset you. Didn't she? You don't have to answer, because I could tell somethin' was wrong...and instinct as well as experience tells me it was Madison. Am I right?"

Ambria felt tears begin to well in her eyes, and so she glanced away from Pike and up into the clear, star-filled sky.

"Tell me the truth now," Pike prodded. "If I'm wrong, I want to know it. But I don't think I am...am I?"

"No...you're not wrong," Ambria admitted. It felt so good to reveal it to him—like she was a pressure cooker and her vent pipe had been allowed to open. "But I've chewed on it long enough today, and I've let it go. I'm more upset now because...I just can't understand how a body could be so mean to her own sister. I mean, she knows I'm still super self-conscious about..."

"About what?" he asked.

Ambria was irritated with herself for letting her mouth run away with her thoughts. "About...about myself," she mumbled, hoping he would not guess exactly what part of herself she was still self-conscious about.

A frown puckered Pike's handsome brows then. "This isn't about your...your...your bosoms again, is it?"

Ambria giggled, entirely amused by his flailing around for a word to refer to her chest and coming up with *bosoms*. It sounded like something her grandmother would say.

"It is, isn't it!" he exclaimed angrily. "That jealous, flat-chested, bottle-blonde bi...beeotch of a sister of yours made fun of your...of you again, didn't she?"

By this time, Ambria was nearly overcome with mirth. Pike's temper was so riled! And yet he was far too amusing for his own good.

"I thought you told me she'd cut that out?" he growled. "I swear, I just wanna wring her neck."

"Me too, sometimes," Ambria admitted. She looked up into his still-glaring blue, blue, bluest eyes, however, and said, "But not right now. Right now, I just want to thank you, again."

"Thank me for what again?" he grumbled, obviously still annoyed.

"Why, for gettin' me through another bad 'Madison moment,' of course. That's what Hadley calls them—Madison moments," she explained. Ambria popped up from her seat on the step just long enough to plant a quick kiss on his five-o'clock-shadowed jaw.

Pike's frown softened—disappeared completely. "At last," he chuckled.

"At last, what?" Ambria asked, puzzled.

"At last you gave me an openin'," he answered.

"An openin'? An openin' to what?" she giggled.

"To this," Pike said.

Ambria giggle-gasped as, all at once, Pike put his arms around her waist, simultaneously standing up and whisking her off the pool steps and into the four-foot and then five-foot depths.

Reflexively, Ambria's arms encircled his neck for support, for at only five-foot-four, the five-foot pool depth would've had her face beneath the water if Pike hadn't been holding her—holding her against the powerful strength of his muscular body.

"See?" he mumbled as he looked directly into her eyes. "Now I've got you right where I want you—you and your perfect, cinnamon-flavored mermaid hair." He grinned and winked at her, adding, "And your perfect mermaid bosoms that your big sister is jealous of. Yep, right where I want you."

"You wanted me in the pool?" Ambria teased. Oh, she sensed what he meant—that he wanted her alone and at a little bit of a disadvantage. Furthermore, she was surprised that his mention of her "perfect mermaid bosoms" hadn't bothered her. Not at all! Any mention of her chest always bothered her, especially from men. But she knew what Pike meant—as a reminder that she had something over Madison, something that made Madison green with envy. She had Pike's attention!

"I want to be alone with you," he said, his voice deep and rich like melted brown sugar. "I'm tired of someone bein' with us every minute of the damn day. Oh sure, we have a sofa here and there we can share, but we've never, ever been all alone. And don't you think it's time we were alone…Ambria?"

"I do," she whispered, breathless by the discernable expression of desire on his handsome face.

"Good," he mumbled. "And so here we are—you, the beautiful, cinnamon-haired mermaid, and me, the dastardly sailor or pirate," he flirted. He quirked one brow, asking, "As a mermaid, which do you prefer I be? A sailor or a pirate?"

Ambria laughed. "Well, sailors are more heroic, aren't they? Aren't pirates more the rogues of the sea? Then again, sailors are rumored to have a girl in every port and…"

"Then pirate it is, love," Pike said in what Ambria deemed the perfect impersonation of a pirate's dialect and accent. "So let's sail around a bit while you get used to the water…and to me holdin' you. What say ye?"

"I say I had no idea you owned such a talent at impersonations, Mr. O'Leary," she answered. "If you ever tire of photographin' crime scenes, I suppose you could always work in the Pirates of the Caribbean ride at Disney."

"Oh, I've talents you have yet to discover, love," Pike chuckled.

Ambria laughed as he walked backward in the pool, pulling her with him—holding her against him. He was quiet for a moment, staring into her eyes with such alluring intensity Ambria was rendered breathless for a time.

"I like this bathing suit you're wearin'," he remarked, having abandoned the pirate accent for the deep, rich, brown-sugar tone that always made Ambria's heart race.

She felt his hands at her waist—at her bare waist—and she stiffened a little, uncomfortable because of her past experiences with men. Still, she trusted Pike. He wasn't like other boys or men she'd dated; she knew he wasn't. He was a gentleman, and he seemed more interested in her face than her chest.

"Why?" she stammered, uncertain as to what else to say.

"Honestly?" he asked.

"Yes," she answered, holding her breath—afraid of what he would say.

"Because you look smokin' hot in it," he admitted, smiling at her. "And there's nothin' wrong with that. And there's nothin' wrong with me sayin' that either. Because I don't have a hidden agenda, Ambria. I'm just bein' honest with you."

For the very first time in her life, Ambria was glad to hear a man tell her she was attractive—that she looked "hot." There was something about the way Pike was looking at her, gazing into her eyes with his blue stare. She could see that he liked her—all of her, not just her figure.

Ambria smiled at him, tightening her embrace around his neck. "Well, you look smokin' hot no matter what you're wearin'," she brazenly divulged.

"Even when I'm half naked, like now?" he flirted with a wink.

"Yes," she admitted. "Even when you're half naked like now."

Pike smiled, and his eyes narrowed, smoldering with such a seductive quality that Ambria felt her stomach leap up into her throat for a moment.

"Well then," he began, "I'm hopin' that the isolation with me, out here in the yellow-jasmine-scented air, with the crickets makin' their romantic music"—there was a quick, soft zap in the air—"and the dulcet tones of various moths and Junebugs meetin' their end in that bug zapper near the awnin'…will afford me the opportunity I've been waitin' for since the moment I saw you at supper the other night at Mancini's."

"What opportunity is that?" Ambria asked—entirely enchanted, charmed, and bewitched by the romantic, provocative spell Pike was spinning her into.

"Oh, sweet cinnamon-haired mermaid of mine," Pike mumbled. "The opportunity to do this, of course."

Pulling Ambria flush against the warmth and protection of his muscular form, Pike slowly moved into deeper water as he pressed a soft, slow kiss to her lips.

"And this," he mumbled, kissing her again. "And this."

With each consecutive kiss, Ambria grew more and more light-headed and breathless. For even though she was accepting of his kisses—even though she joined him in the kisses, pursing her lips against his, reveling in the knowledge Pike O'Leary was kissing her, blissful in the physical pleasure his kiss provoked in her—she held back, afraid of untethering her reserve, of letting go of her instincts to protect her emotions, her heart.

"And now this," Pike said as his arms banded around her, one strong hand resting at the back of her neck, the other firmly supporting her at her waist.

It was the end of any doubt or inhibition—any shred of self-preservation Ambria had left in her. As Pike's warm, cinnamon-zested mouth claimed hers in an irresistible, exquisitely enforced, and thoroughly visceral kiss, Ambria melted against him—allowed her hands to caress the back of his neck—ran her fingers up into his soft cocoa-colored hair. It was clear Pike approved of her response, for his kiss intensified, demanding like reciprocation—and Ambria complied, smoothly fisting his hair in her hands.

The instant, synchronized, perfect rhythm of their shared kisses astounded Ambria but led her mind to silently decreeing, *You love him! You love him! And he's the only man you ever will love!* And although the secret revelation to herself caused near overwhelming emotion to gather as tears in her eyes, Ambria was not deterred. No matter what may come—if Pike continued to see her once the wedding was over or if to him this was just a best man and maid of honor fling thing—Ambria surrendered to the moment, returning Pike's masterful kisses with as much impulsive, impassioned wantonness as he gave them.

After Ambria had no idea how long, Pike eventually broke the seal of their mouths, leaning back to study her face and smiling at her. Ambria blushed. It was an unnerving thing to have such an incredible man study her so closely—so intimately.

Once more, Pike began to move them around the pool, and as he did so he began to hum. Ambria recognized the melody of the song he was humming after only a few measures.

"Are you...are you hummin' 'It's You I Like'?" she giggled. "The Mr. Rogers' 'It's You I Like' song?"

"Yes, ma'am," Pike confirmed, grinning at her. "It's been runnin' through my head almost nonstop since that night at Mancini's. Every time I think of you, that ol' Mr. Rogers' song starts up."

Ambria giggled, biting her lower lip a little with amusement. "Well, am I to be flattered by the fact that when you see me you start thinkin' about PBS children's show tunes? Or not?"

Pike placed a kiss at the corner of Ambria's mouth, and goose bumps raced over her arms and legs.

"Let me tell you somethin', darlin'," he began. "This world would be a much better place if people still raised their kids on *Mr. Rogers' Neighborhood* and *Sesame Street*. And this country would be a lot smarter if people made certain their kids were watchin' *Schoolhouse Rock* every afternoon instead of playin' video games."

"I wholeheartedly agree," Ambria assured him. "But I'm still not sure I should be flattered that I inspire Mr. Rogers' songs where you're concerned."

"Well, think of the words," Pike offered. "A song all about likin' someone for who they are...not what they own or what they wear." He paused, winking at Ambria and adding, "Although what you're wearin' right now...I like it." Ambria blushed, and Pike continued.

"I like you, Ambria, everything about you. So, yes, you should be flattered that Mr. Rogers' song is runnin' through my head. Because I really do like you…really, really like you."

"Well, then, I'm glad Mr. Rogers is runnin' through your head…because I really, really like you too."

Pike smiled. "Good ol' Mr. Rogers. I love that dude," he chuckled.

"Me too," Ambria affectionately acknowledged.

Pike continued to hum, and even sometimes sing, "It's You I Like" as he moved them around the pool. And Ambria continued to fall deeper and deeper in love with the most gorgeous, beefcaked, super-stud lady-killer, Mr. Rogers admirer she'd ever seen.

"You need to promise me that you'll have our kids watch Mr. Rogers every mornin' before school, all right?" Pike dropped all at once.

Although Ambria's heart felt like it leapt up and almost out of her nose at his inference they would have children together one day, she succeeded in keeping the appearance of calm on the outside.

"Of course," she managed. "Was there ever any question that they wouldn't?"

Pike smiled and hummed a few more bars of "It's You I Like," before pulling Ambria to him and returning to his previous endeavors of lavishing her with delicious emotional and physical pleasure. And as she savored his kiss—bathed in the beautiful bliss of his affections—Ambria knew she would never, ever be the same.

♥

As Harmony and Charlie stood gazing out onto the patio—as they stared at Pike and Ambria stretched out together on a patio lounger and fast asleep in each other's arms—Harmony sighed with delight.

"Well, I'm guessin' things went well," Charlie said, mirthfully stating the obvious.

"I'm guessin' it did indeed," Harmony whispered. Her heart soared with joy at seeing her most beloved friend being held tight in the arms of a man like Pike O'Leary.

Turning to Charlie, Harmony took his face between her hands, kissing him squarely on the mouth. "It's meant to be, Charlie," she quietly exclaimed as tears filled her eyes. "Me and you...we were meant to be. And we were meant to bring Ambria and Pike together. They were meant to be too...I just know it!"

Charlie—always the voice of reason, yet never the deflator of hope—smiled at Harmony, saying, "Well, it certainly appears that they're on the path to it. It certainly does."

Harmony's heart warmed at the way Charlie had of always encouraging her and yet trying to prepare her for her dreams being dashed. He was so wonderful!

"I love you so much, Charlie Oaks," she said as tears filled her eyes—tears of joy in knowing she would soon be his wife.

Charlie chuckled, "Well, I certainly hope so, darlin'!" He kissed her and then glanced back out to the patio where Pike and Ambria were fast asleep together. "So should we wake them up or what?"

"Oh, for pity's sake, of course not!" Harmony assured him. "For the highly intelligent man that you are, you sure do ask some silly questions. Now let's go, before they wake up and see us standin' here watchin' them like a couple of perverts."

"Perverts?" Charlie quietly laughed. "Well, they ain't doin' nothin' but sleepin'...so how does that make us perverts?"

"Oh, you know perfectly well what I meant. They need their privacy," Harmony explained.

"Yes, ma'am, Mrs. Oaks," Charlie said. "Whatever you say, Mrs. Oaks. I'll do anything you ask, Mrs. Oaks."

As Charlie continued to tease her as they headed for the entertainment room, Harmony's heart swelled with indescribable happiness—for not only was she about to marry the man of her dreams in Charlie, but it looked like Ambria would soon follow suit with Pike. *Oh, it just has to work out between Ambria and Pike,* Harmony silently determined. It just had to! And after all, what on earth could possibly interfere?

CHAPTER SIX

Pike could not keep from staring at Ambria. Every time she walked across the room, talked with someone, laughed, smiled—he could not tear his gaze away from her. He'd never known anything as wonderful, as comfortable; nothing had ever seemed so "meant to be" or felt so right as waking up with her in his arms at four a.m. that morning. Sure, sleeping on the patio lounger for several hours had made his back sore. But he didn't give a damn. Because holding Ambria in his arms for those hours, waking to the feel of her soft, rhythmic breathing as she lay against his chest, was worth any pain or discomfort. And their time spent kissing in the pool? Pike felt goose bumps prickle his arms at the memory. Ambria was the one. As he watched her walking toward the table where he was sitting— as he watched her smile broaden as she drew closer to him, staring at him with those honey-brown eyes that made his stomach flip-flop—he knew she was the one.

All at once, however, as fate always seemed to have it, realization leapt to his mind, and he wondered when he should tell Ambria about his past. Previously, Pike had determined to wait until after Charlie and Harmony's wedding. After all, it was their time, their special day, and he didn't want anything infringing on the joy they deserved to relish. Still, he knew he had to tell Ambria, especially before things got any more serious between them—which he was determined they would. And so Pike's delight in studying Ambria as she sat down in the chair next to him was tainted—tainted by his past, tainted by the worry deep inside him that the woman he had fallen in love with would turn and run from him as fast as her cute little feet could carry her once all was revealed.

"Combinin' the bachelorette and bachelor party to just one big party for their friends was a great idea on Harmony and Charlie's part!" Ambria noted with a smile. "What a great party, right?"

Pike chuckled, leaned over, and kissed her on the cheek. "What?" he asked. "You're not categorizin' it as a 'gag-therin'?"

Ambria's heart leapt inside her as Pike draped his arm along the back of her chair. "Nope," she giggled. "So I guess miracles do happen every day." She gazed at Pike, her heart feeling like it might jump right out of her chest. He was so wonderful! So perfect to her—for her.

"I can't believe you still remember that," she laughed.

"Remember it?" Pike exclaimed. "It's run through my mind at every social event I've ever attended since. It's perfect!"

"It's run through your mind at every social event since because that night at supper with my family four years ago was so traumatizin' to you," Ambria teased.

But Pike's eyes narrowed, smoldering with emotion. "That night four years ago ended up bein' the greatest night of my life…'cause I met you that night," he said in a low voice, rich with emotion.

"My, my, my, Mr. O'Leary," Ambria whispered, leaning close to him. "You are such a charmer."

"I try," Pike said. Reaching out, he cupped her chin in his hand, placing a soft, lingering kiss to her mouth.

"You succeed," Ambria breathed, letting her arms slide around his neck as she returned his kiss.

She couldn't believe it! She was sitting there kissing Pike O'Leary—in public! And she didn't care! She didn't care if someone saw them kissing. In fact, she hoped that they did! Ambria silently scolded herself as the thought darted into her mind that she hoped Madison, in particular, saw them kissing. It was a selfish, malicious sort of thought, so Ambria tried to push it from her thoughts. And fortunately the effect of Pike's kiss helped to disperse it—rendering her mind blank of any awareness other than the fact that he existed, that he was marvelous, and that he had chosen her to kiss.

"All right, all right," Harmony interrupted. "You guys can get a room later. Right now, I need Ambria to get ready. It's almost time for our presentation of my weddin' gift to Charlie."

"Oh, I'm sure the only weddin' gift Charlie's hopin' for is the one you can give him once you two are safely tucked away in your honeymoon suite Saturday night," Pike said as he pulled back from Ambria.

"Do not be naughty, Pike," Harmony giggled with a good sense of humor. "And give me my friend. It's almost time." Taking Ambria's hand, Harmony pulled her to her feet. Then conspiratorially winking at Pike, she added, "And you might want to get a front-row seat at the groom and groomsmen table over there, Pike O'Leary. 'Cause the way you two were lockin' lips just now, I'm sure you're goin' to enjoy our performance almost as much as Charlie will!"

"Well, you've got me intrigued now, Harmony," Pike said, winking at Ambria.

"See you," Ambria said.

"Oh, you can count on it," Pike told her, smiling.

♥

"I'm so nervous," Harmony whispered to Ambria as they waited for Charlie's brothers to set up the two-by-three-foot-square wood mats she and her bridesmaids would need for their performance.

"Why?" Ambria asked. "We could do this number with our eyes closed."

"You and Kayla and me could," Harmony agreed. "But it was an awful lot for Jordan, Brooke, Sierra, and Chelsea to learn. Oh, why didn't I just keep my gift for Charlie simple?"

Placing an arm of reassurance around Harmony's waist, Ambria consoled, "Because Charlie loves to watch you Irish step dancin'. Why, I swear his eyes light up like lightnin' bug bums when he watches you dance. And you want to please him, give him somethin' truly memorable. Besides, the girls will do fine. You and me and Kayla will step the hardest part. The others mostly keep the rhythm and add to the tap volume. Furthermore, they know it, they've worked hard on learnin' the bit we could teach them, and they're excited to do it for you and Charlie. No more worries, okay?"

Harmony exhaled a heavy sigh, smiling at Ambria. "You're right, of course," she agreed. "Charlie will love it! Thanks, Am."

"I'm only tellin' you the truth. No need to thank me for that," Ambria reminded her.

"Well, here goes nothin' then," Harmony said as they heard Charlie's brother announce that it was time for Harmony and her bridesmaids to present the groom's gift.

Someone started the music, and the percussion intro of "Irish Party in Third Class" by Gaelic Storm began to play. Harmony giggled when she heard Charlie begin to hoot and holler with approval, excitement, and delight.

"See? He already loves it!" Ambria laughed.

Following Harmony out to the large entertainment room of the house, Ambria, Harmony, and Kayla began their Irish step dancing routine on their individual wooden mats placed directly in front of the groom's table. Jordan, Brooke, Sierra, and Chelsea took their places on the wooden mats just behind them, joining in with a simpler step.

Instantly, Ambria's heart soared as the beat of her own hard shoes on the wooden mat began to ring in her ears in time with the music. She loved dancing, especially step dancing. She'd watched a DVD of the original Riverdance when she was just three years old, and it had inspired her first dream: to become an Irish step dancer. She'd thought age five (when Irish dancing classes started for children in Charleston) would never arrive—but it eventually had. Through Irish dancing, Ambria had found not only her very first love but also her very best friend, Harmony.

As it was anytime she performed, Ambria's heart began to race with excitement. How she loved the rhythmic, synchronized tap sound of the dancers' hard shoes! How she loved the feel of the long banana curls of her auburn hair bouncing as she danced, loved the feel of the hem of her short black lace dress swishing against her thighs, the black lace sleeves against her arms. And then—then she looked from Charlie to Pike, and her heart began to beat even faster. Pike sat in his chair at the groom's table looking absolutely astonished. His eyes were as wide as Ambria's mama's china supper plates, and his mouth was even gaping open a little.

She giggled to herself, realizing that he had no idea she was an Irish step dancer. By the awed expression on his face, as he joined in clapping in rhythm with everyone else at the party, Ambria could see he approved—very much approved.

"Holy shhh…Charlie!" Pike exclaimed to his friend. "You never told me they could do…this!"

Charlie laughed, "It's how Harmony and Ambria met, dude! As little girls in Irish dance school!" Nudging Pike with one elbow, he added, "Are you turned on or what? Ambria ain't got a chance of gettin' away from you now, no matter what, does she?"

"No, indeed," Pike agreed. "She ain't got a chance in hell of escapin' me now."

Pike sat enthralled as he watched Ambria dance. His heart was beating so hard and so fast he was certain it would do the *Alien* and bust right out of his chest at any moment! He wouldn't have believed there was anything in the world that could make Ambria Blanchard even more attractive to him than she already was! And then she steps out in a short lacy black dress, long cinnamon-hair curls cascading from her head, and wearing Irish tap shoes. Pile on that, she could Irish dance like she'd stepped right out of the old Riverdance troupe, and Pike had to keep from drooling like a Neanderthal as he watched her!

"Dude! Don't have a heart attack," Charlie chuckled.

"I'm tryin' not to," Pike admitted.

Pike smiled as he watched the woman he loved perform a very difficult, very impressive dance routine. He was awed, he was euphoric, he was tingly! He was even a little embarrassed, because when he thought about what Charlie had planned for his wedding gift to Harmony—well, Pike knew his, Charlie's, and the other groomsmen's performance would be pathetic compared with what the girls were doing. But still, wasn't that the way it often went? Men may be born with focus and steadfastness, but women were born overachievers.

As the music began to speed up, signaling the impending finale of the song and performance, Charlie leapt to his feet, not only clapping in rhythm now but also stomping one foot in rhythm too. Understanding it was a premature standing ovation, Pike quickly stood as well, adding his own stomp to the rhythm.

And when it ended, when everyone in the room began to whistle and applaud with approval, Pike followed suit as Charlie climbed over the table and headed straight for Harmony. Only Pike wasn't headed for Harmony. He was headed for the delicious cinnamon-haired beauty who had won him over lock, stock, and barrel.

As Charlie picked up Harmony, whirling her around in expressing his approval of her gift—his pleasure in it—Pike grabbed ahold of Ambria's arm, pulling her to one side.

Ambria smiled as Pike took her face between his warm, strong hands, staring down into her face. He was so handsome it made her mouth water!

"Are you even kiddin' me?" he asked in a rather breathless-sounding tone. "I mean, holy shh…I mean…oh my h…oh my…my giddy aunt! You're an Irish dance girl? Every fantasy I ever had as a teenager involved an Irish dancin' girl! You've just made all my dreams come true, Ambria Blanchard!"

Ambria giggled, entirely enchanted by the pure admiration in Pike's eyes as he looked at her. "Well, I'm happy to oblige, sir," she teased.

"Get over here," Pike mumbled, tugging on her arm again—pulling her behind the large blackout draperies that led to the theater room.

No sooner had he sequestered her into privacy, isolating them from the rest of the partiers, then she was in his arms. Ambria giggled again, goose bumps racing over every inch of her body as Pike proceeded to smother her with kisses. He kissed her face, her neck, the top of her head, her hands, her wrists.

At last she pushed his hands from her face, taking his in hers. "Right here, buddy," Ambria said. Pursing her lips, she made a kissing sound with them. "Quit wastin' my time, and kiss me like—"

Ambria didn't even finish what she was saying—she couldn't! In an instant she was wrapped in Pike's powerful arms, bound against his muscular body as his mouth worked such a rapturous bliss to hers that she thought for a moment she might faint! It was as if she couldn't kiss him hard enough—or thoroughly enough—or just plain enough!

Suddenly appearing as he pulled aside the blackout curtains, Charlie said, "Well, at least you're not suckin' on her hair this time, dude. Come on! We're up!"

Breaking the seal of their mouths, Pike gazed into Ambria's eyes. She was lost in the blue, blue, blue of them as he mumbled, "We're up."

"Okay," she breathed, still caught in such a whirl of euphoria that it took her a few seconds to realize what he was talking about.

"Once you get your knees steadied again, Ambria," Charlie chuckled, "get to that table in your seat and prepare yourself for our hotness!"

"Okay," Ambria giggle-breathed. It was sinking in now—the fact that Charlie and his groomsmen had prepared something as a gift for Harmony.

"I am goin' to eat you alive when I get through here, pussycat," Pike said with a wink as Charlie took hold of his arm and literally dragged him away.

Ambria laughed, biting her lip with amused pleasure at Pike's threat of further affection.

Trying to appear as unruffled as possible after her encounter with Pike behind the drapes, Ambria made her way to the table where Charlie, Pike, and the other groomsmen had watched Harmony and her bridesmaids dance.

"Did you survive bein' ravished by Pike?" Harmony asked with a wink as Ambria sat down in the chair next to her.

"I think, barely," Ambria admitted—still awash in bliss because of Pike's kiss.

"Oh, I love you two together, Am!" Harmony exclaimed in a whisper.

"Me too," Ambria sighed.

"And the look on your big sister's face just now," Harmony continued, "when she saw the way Pike went after you like a hound dog catchin' scent of a fox..." Harmony's smile broadened. "Mm-mmm! I loved it!"

"Madison?" Ambria asked. In truth, she'd entirely forgotten her sister was in attendance at the party at all.

"Of course Madison!" Harmony assured. "Why, she was as green as a tomato worm! It was wonderful!"

Initially Ambria felt the ugly imp of prideful gloating begin to rise in her chest. But then her common sense kicked in. And if there was one thing her common sense knew about Madison, it was that if Madison were at all envious of the fact that Ambria had captured Pike's attention and affections, then there would be hell to pay— eventually.

Still, Ambria was too high on cloud nine to worry about any "Madison moments" that might come her way in the future. For she'd felt something in Pike's kiss—something new and reassuring.

Oh sure, she'd felt desire from him—felt he liked her—just as she'd felt it from him the night before in the pool. But this time, Ambria was certain she'd felt something even more wonderful. This time she was sure she felt he loved her! As impossible as it sounded, even to herself, she had sensed that Pike O'Leary loved her—or in the very least that he was beginning to.

"And now, Harmony," Kayla began to announce, "Charlie has a gift for you too! Presentin' Charlie Oaks and his groomsmen!"

The moment the music began, the moment the profoundly recognizable intro to Vanilla Ice's "Ice Ice Baby" began—even before Charlie and his groomsmen entered the room wearing the iconic black harem-style pants popularized by MC Hammer and Vanilla Ice in the early 1990s—Harmony was out of her seat and squealing as she jumped up and down with excitement.

Thoroughly elated herself, Ambria leapt out of her seat, her cheeks hurting from the intensity of the sight of Pike dressed in the harem pants and loose-fitting white shirt he and the others were wearing. As Pike and the others proceeded to perform an incredibly authentic hip-hop-style dance and lip-sync impersonation of Vanilla Ice and his "crew," Ambria squealed with delight! She knew Harmony was loving the performance to one of her favorite vintage songs, but Ambria was also certain that she couldn't possibly be enjoying it as much as Ambria was, for Pike was spot on—perfect! If she hadn't known better, she would've thought he was somehow channeling the classic vanilla rapper.

And then, just when Ambria thought the performance by Pike and the groomsmen couldn't get any more superb and affecting, Charlie hollered, "Ice!" Having cued his friends, Charlie and his groomsmen proceeded to strip off their shirts in one smooth motion, revealing black bow ties at their throats. Harmony, Ambria, and the other bridesmaids giggled and applauded in unison, while the other partygoers whistled and catcalled.

As if she weren't already light-headed with butterflies swarming in her stomach and her heart hammering with the force of a professional drumline, Ambria squealed with appreciation as she watched Pike finish out the performance with flawless hip-hop skill.

Too soon, the performance was over, and everyone was applauding and calling out compliments. But all at once, Ambria understood Pike's reaction to having seen her dance. And careless of what her hard shoes might do to the tabletop, Ambria followed Harmony over it and raced toward Pike.

"Oh my...giddy aunt!" she laughed as she reached him. Throwing her arms around his neck, she confessed, "I just want to eat you alive, pussycat!"

Panting a little from the exertion of the dance, Pike laughed, gathering her into his arms.

"Oh, so you're a Vanilla Ice fan too, huh?" he asked, kissing her on the cheek.

"I'm a Pike O'Leary fan," she corrected him, tiptoeing and placing a kiss on his chin.

"I sure hope so," he said, kissing her square on the mouth.

"Oh my! You are all just so talented!" a young woman who had been pointed out to Ambria earlier as the wife of one of Charlie's friends exclaimed as she approached. "The girls and the boys! This has got to be the most amazin' weddin' party ever assembled— truly!"

"Thank you," Harmony accepted graciously.

And then, before Ambria could even think to pull Pike toward the blackout curtains and into privacy, a mob of party attendees descended on everyone, hurling compliments and stealing hugs of approval. Although she was disappointed that the cloud of attendees had thwarted her plans to pull Pike into isolation with her so that they could pick up where'd they'd left off, she knew that the party would be winding down soon. Charlie and Harmony had planned to present their "gifts" to one another as a kind of finale of the evening. Therefore, Ambria figured she'd have Pike all to herself again soon enough. She could be patient. Well, she had to be patient anyway.

♥

Sure enough, about half an hour after Charlie and his groomsmen had finished their performance, people started saying their goodbyes and taking their leave. It had been an epic party, one that Ambria had thoroughly enjoyed. But her proverbial purse had been emptied, and the fatigue an empty purse always left her with was starting to set in. As she watched a few people offering their well-wishes to Harmony and Charlie, as well as thanking them for a wonderful evening, Ambria thought of the night before—of falling asleep in Pike's arms on the patio lounge chair.

She exhaled a heavy sigh but not of fatigue—a sigh of wishing she could relive that circumstance over and over, falling asleep in Pike's arms.

"I bet you're worn out, huh?" Madison said, smiling as she approached Ambria.

All at once Ambria was too tired to even listen to the *Shields up! Enemy approaching!* prompt from her internal alarm system.

"I am," Ambria answered. "And I won't deny it."

"And I see you and Pike have cozied up nice and tight already," Madison remarked.

A voice in her mind shouted, *Take evasive action! Evade! Evade!* But Ambria thought that surely Madison wouldn't choose that very moment—Charlie and Harmony's party—to release her envious wrath.

So she answered, "Yep."

"Sooo…I guess he hasn't told you anything about…about what happened then. About what he what he did to that girl?" Madison dropped.

Pike looked up from talking with some old friends of his and Charlie's—looked up to where Ambria stood talking to her sister, Madison. Instantly, his heart dropped with a thud to the bottom of his stomach, for he could tell by the look on Madison Blanchard's face that she was about to deliver a blow to her sister. And Pike wouldn't stand for it, not anymore. Ambria was the one for him—he knew it—and he would do all he could to protect her from the malice her older sister always seemed to sling at Ambria when she was least expecting it.

"Excuse me a minute," Pike mumbled to his friends as he headed toward Ambria and Madison.

Reaching the two women, Pike didn't waste any time enacting a defensive posture, for he knew—instinctively knew—that she was up to no good.

"And what are you up to tonight, Madison?" he asked flatly.

"Me?" Madison asked, feigning innocence. "Why, nothin' at all, Pike. Nothin' at all. Just tryin' to save my little sister from ruinin' her life by gettin' involved with a rapist."

"What?" Ambria gasped then.

The nausea that was all too familiar to Pike gripped his stomach. It had been a while since he'd endured it—but he and that sickening nausea were well acquainted.

"Ambria," he began, taking hold of Ambria's arm, "I knew I should've talked to you about this…but I was tryin' to wait until after the weddin' and—"

"You see, Ambria," Madison interrupted, "it's true. While he was in college, he drugged a girl, had nonconsensual relations with her, and even got her pregnant." Glaring at Pike with the eyes of a witch—a jealous, malicious witch—Madison added, "And it's not a secret, is it, Pike? It's public record."

"Madison! What is wrong with you?" Ambria asked. Looking to Pike, taking hold of his arm, she said, "Pike, I know my sister, and I know there's more to this than she's tellin' me. So—"

Pike wrenched his arm out of Ambria's grasp, leveled an index finger at Madison, and said, "I'm too angry to deal with you now, Madison. So I'll bid you to stay out of my way for a time."

"Pike, I researched this for myself," Madison calmly stated. "And I am determined to keep my sister safe."

"Stay out of my way, Madison," Pike growled. "I mean it."

Ambria could visibly see the deep, excruciating pain in her lover's eyes! There was obviously something to what Madison was accusing him of. And yet Ambria knew it wasn't true—knew it couldn't be true. She knew Pike's heart and soul—had known it for four years. But she could see the rage welling in him, as well.

And when he looked at her, saying, "Give me some time, Ambria. I just need some time. I'll be back in a while," she simply nodded and let him go—watched him storm away.

Ambria felt sick as she watched Pike leave her—watched him push people aside as he headed for the front door and escape.

And when he did escape, slamming the door behind him, Madison said, "'You see there? I just saved your life, little sister.

There he goes, runnin' off like the rapist dog that he is…with his tail between his legs."

CHAPTER SEVEN

Ambria wanted to chase after Pike—to run after him and tell him that she knew there was more to the sordid accusations Madison was making than she knew. But she didn't go after him, for something deep in her heart told her to let him go—that he needed some space. He had said he'd be back, said he needed some time, and so Ambria somehow managed to hold her position and not go chasing after him.

"If his reaction isn't evidence enough of the fact that he did it, then I don't know what more you want," Madison snidely commented.

Gulping down the fear that had lumped in her throat as she'd watched Pike go—let him go—Ambria gritted her teeth with fury as she turned, glaring at her sister.

"What is wrong with you, Madison?" she growled.

"Me?" Madison exclaimed, her face expressing shock and offense. "What is wrong with me? I'm the one who just saved your whole life, Ambria! If he'd pulled you any further into his web—"

"There's more to the story, Madison. I feel it in my soul!" Ambria scolded in a whisper. After all, Charlie and Harmony still had party guests present, as well as other bridesmaids and groomsmen who were staying at the house.

"Oh, don't go on about feelin' it in your soul again," Madison growled with rage. "I am so sick of your soul feelin' everything. And if it feels so much as you claim it does, why didn't it feel the truth about Pike O'Leary, hmm? You've known him, what? A week? Isn't that long enough for your clairvoyant soul to feel that he's a devil?"

"I've known him a lot longer than a week," Ambria informed her sister. "I've known him…felt him for four years. I've just kept you ignorant to it." As her animosity toward her sister continued to heighten, Ambria added, "And believe me, ignorance comes easy to you, so it wasn't hard to keep you in the dark about Pike."

Madison's eyes were red with indignation and outrage. "I am not ignorant, Ambria! You know I'm—"

"I know you were raised in the same house with the same parents and the same rules that Hadley and I were…but you're nothin' like us!" Ambria interrupted. "If you were, you would've been more sensitive to your feelin's and suspected somethin' happened between me and Pike that night four years ago. But you're not sensitive like me and Hadley! You're mean and—"

"What happened four years ago?" It was Madison's turn to interrupt. "Are you talkin' about the night I brought Pike home for supper and you got all upset about me teasin' you about your boobs?" Madison puffed a breath of indifference. "I paid for that for years, Ambria. Believe me, Mama and Daddy made sure of it. Furthermore, you and your simperin' martyr's expression sent Pike runnin' for the hills! He never did talk to me after supper that night!"

"Well, he talked to me," Ambria stated.

"What? What are you talkin' about?" Madison demanded. "What do you mean he talked to you afterward?"

Then Ambria let it out: the secret she'd kept to herself for so long—the tender, treasured memory of Pike's profound encouragement that night. It was time to share it—to let Madison know the truth.

"Maybe you remember that I didn't stay at the table for dessert that night," Ambria began. "I was too upset by how you had made fun of me in front of Pike and the family…so I left and took Chunk for a walk."

"So?" Madison prodded.

"So when I came walkin' back toward the house, Pike was there…waitin' for me. For me, Madison," she confessed. And as she did, her heart swelled with the full understanding that it was that night four years before when she'd first fallen in love with Pike—and somehow the knowledge served to soften her heart toward her sister. Miraculous as it was, Ambria softened—became conscious again that Madison's malice was spurred by jealousy, not hatred of Ambria.

"What?" Madison breathed.

"He was there," Ambria continued. "He'd waited for me, waited so he could tell me not to let you make me feel bad about myself anymore. He told me you were a bully and not to let you do it anymore. And so I didn't. From that night on, I stood up to you…because Pike found enough interest in me, enough value in me, to wait and give me the most encouragin' 'pep talk' of my life, outside of Mama and Daddy. It's why he never had anything to do with you after that—because you were so mean to me, not because I had worn an expression of martyrdom as you claim."

Madison was quiet for a moment, her glare so fierce that it made Ambria's teeth hot.

"Well, he's still a date-raper and a dead-beat father," Madison murmured.

"No, he's not." It was Charlie's voice Ambria heard behind her.

Madison looked past Ambria and then to Charlie, accusing, "Yes, he is. I Googled him. And you're the one who was goin' to let my sister walk right into his trap."

"You need to go home now, Madison," Harmony said as she stepped up next to Ambria and placed an arm around her shoulders. Oh, Harmony sounded calm—but Ambria knew it was just her hostess voice speaking. Had there not been other people around, Harmony would've torn into Madison like a starving hyena to a carcass. "I'll call you tomorrow to make sure all is well with the flowers. But for now, you need to leave…to go home."

"Yep. You do need to go home," Charlie growled. "You need to go home and Google Pike a little further than you obviously did—for you made a mess of it, woman. You didn't get at the truth at all…just sucked on the nasty rumors. Please leave."

Madison's face turned a shade of crimson humiliation that Ambria was certain was painful to her.

"Fine," Madison said. "I will do just that, Charlie Oaks. But what I read and how far I research won't change the facts."

"No, you're right," Charlie agreed. "It sure won't. But you be sure you have facts in hand, as well as an apology for Pike, before I see you again, woman."

Madison was seething! Her eyes narrowed as she glared at Charlie.

"And I'm assumin' you know about Charlie's involvement in everything that happened with the druggin' and the date rape and—" Madison began.

"Oh, I know all about Charlie's involvement in what did and did not happen that night, Madison," Harmony stated. "And now, again…I'll call you tomorrow. Please leave."

Madison shot one last glare at Ambria. "You should be thankin' me, Ambria," she said. "I hope someday, when you've got your head screwed back on straight, you'll understand that I tried to save you tonight."

"Goodbye, Madison," Ambria said flatly.

"Bye now," Madison said. Then she turned and rather arrogantly sashayed toward the front door.

Once Ambria had watched her sister close the door behind her, she turned to Charlie, tears spilling from her eyes.

"What is this all about, Charlie?" she quietly cried. "Please...I know there's more to the story, and Pike is obviously devastated about whatever it is. But please, don't leave me just standin' here in agony until he gets back and we can talk! If you know it all...please, please tell me!"

"I had no idea it was Pike that you went through all that with, Charlie," Harmony whispered, reaching out to caress her fiancé's cheek.

"Nope, you didn't," Charlie admitted. "Pike went through hell that year, and I didn't ever want him to have to see pity in your eyes when you look at him, Harm. He hates that."

"What happened, Charlie?" Ambria begged again. Her heart was beating so hard with anxiety and stress—worry for Pike's well-being—that she could hardly breathe! She was determined to look for him, to search wherever she had to for as long as she had to in order to find him and console him—reassure him that she loved him and knew he could never have done what Madison was claiming he did. But first she needed more information—more insight into what had happened and why Pike was so upset.

Charlie nodded. "Um...why don't you go on and wait in your bedroom, Ambria? Let me and Harmony get everyone out the door and settled. Then I promise I'll come up and tell you what I can. It's Pike's story to tell you, his pain to share, but I know you need to know now. So run on into your room and wait." Charlie smiled at her with assurance, even for the pain that was now evident in his eyes.

"Okay," Ambria agreed, brushing tears from her cheeks. "Okay."

And with that, she hurried to the bedroom she was sharing with Harmony, all the while praying for Pike's well-being and that the remaining guests would take their leave as quickly as possible.

♥

"I've always blamed myself for what happened," Charlie began.

"You shouldn't, darlin'," Harmony whispered, placing a hand on his shoulder with reassurance.

"Well, I have," Charlie reiterated. "After all, it was my stupid idea to pledge a fraternity."

"What happened, Charlie?" Ambria prodded. "Tell me…please."

Ambria had waited in her room as Charlie had asked her to. Yet it had been a long wait, waiting for Charlie to explain everything, worrying over Pike until she was sick to her stomach. She'd changed into some comfortable shorts and a T-shirt, but that had only taken moments. Finally, after the longest twenty minutes of her life, Charlie and Harmony had managed to get all their party guests out the door. Now Charlie sat next to Ambria on the small love seat in the bedroom. Harmony sat on its arm, lovingly stroking Charlie's hair to soothe him.

Charlie cleared his throat, shifting uncomfortably in his seat. "Well, I'll give you the gist of it, at least. Pike can tell you the whole sordid story when he gets back." Charlie paused, lowering his eyes with guilt. "He'll want to tell you all the gory details himself. I know he's wanted to tell you all before now, but he was tryin' to wait until after the weddin'. But when he gets back...he can tell you everything."

Ambria frowned with worry. Charlie looked at her, his eyes wet with emotion—with regret. "He will be back, Ambria," he assured her. "He will. He's just...whenever it comes up—and it seems it always will come up at one time or another—it just brings back a lot of pain, frustration, and anger. He'll process it though, and then he'll be back." Charlie shrugged and shook his head, adding, "Although I'm sure he won't set eyes on your sister for a long, long time...not after this."

Ambria nodded, understanding why Pike would resent Madison and trying to believe Charlie's assurance that Pike was just processing the renewed pain of an old wound. Ambria felt her jaw clench with fury as she thought of what Madison had done—or tried to do, at least. Even so, Ambria silently prayed that Pike would come back—and soon.

"I understand," she affirmed. Ambria was so impatient, desperate to know what had happened to Pike—desperate for him to come back so she could help him. Yet she could see Charlie struggling as well. And so she tried to be patient.

Charlie nodded. "Okay," he mumbled in agreement. "Okay."

Ambria exchanged worried glances with Harmony. It was apparent Harmony had some knowledge about whatever it was that had happened—what Madison stumbled upon that gave her the gall to tell her Pike was an accused rapist and possibly had a child. But she could also see that Harmony was being careful not to push Charlie too hard, and Ambria understood why. No woman wanted to see the man she loved in pain. Harmony didn't want to see

Charlie hurting, just like Ambria didn't want to see Pike hurting. Yet she thought that she would prefer to have him there with her while he was, so at least she could attempt to comfort him.

"So when we started college, I came up with this bright idea that me and Pike should pledge one of the fraternities," Charlie began, his shoulders sagging, his head hanging with the weight of a difficult memory. "Pike wasn't all in. He didn't have a high regard for the frat life. He didn't really have any interest in pledgin'. But I was bent on it, and as always, Pike was supportive. So we pledged. Of course the hazin' and all was asinine. Nothin' but partyin' and bein' humiliated every wakin' minute of the day and night. The entire situation was just plain stupid, and Pike kept tellin' me we should cut our losses and run." Charlie paused, shaking his head and rubbing at his whisker stubble. "But I wanted to stick it out. And so we hung in there a bit longer. The whole damn thing was worse for Pike. He took a lot of grief because he wasn't a true partier, you know? More even than I did…a lot more, for some reason. They called us both 'square losers' and all 'cause we wouldn't smoke weed or drink copious amounts of alcohol the way they all did. But for some reason, they were harder on Pike. And I figure that what happened—what caused it all to go straight to hell—was that some frat boy took it personally that Pike wasn't 'all in,' so to speak. Or else he was jealous of Pike—there're plenty for reasons for a man to be envious of Pike O'Leary. Anyway, one night there was a big party at our frat house, and it was out of control from the minute it started. Everybody was boozin' it up, doin' drugs; everything that gives frat parties a bad name was goin' on. Of course, Pike wasn't down with any of it. He just kept drinkin' a steady stream of cherry cola, and me and him were standin' around just in awe of how depraved these college kids could be, you know?"

"Yeah," Harmony prodded, stroking Charlie's hair at the back of his neck to comfort him.

"Well, the best we can figure," Charlie continued, "and we still don't know how or when it happened…but somebody spiked Pike's cherry cola at some point…roofied it. Because about midnight, all of a sudden he started feelin' really sick to his stomach and dizzy. It was bad! He was slurrin' when he talked and could hardly walk. For a minute, I wondered if maybe he'd decided to try the booze that was everywhere, 'cause by the time I helped him get back up to our room, he had thrown up twice and was ready to pass out. He got some vomit on his shirt, so I helped him get out of his clothes, all but his drawers, and not a moment too soon. 'Cause next thing I knew, he face-planted onto the bed and was out cold. By that time, I wasn't feelin' too good myself, so I went into the bathroom to take care of some business, you know? And I swear, I wasn't gone more than three or four minutes—but when I came out, there was this girl…this strange girl in bed with Pike. Pike was lyin' just like I left him, laid out flat on his stomach, completely unconscious. But…but…somehow this girl had made it into our room, and she was…she was stripped down to nothin' and lyin' on the bed next to him."

Ambria gulped down the nausea rising in her throat. The story Charlie was relating had just gone from sickening to horrifying! Yet she didn't say a word—just sat waiting for Charlie to go on.

Charlie raked his fingers back through his hair. "I feel sick to my stomach just thinkin' on all this again," he mumbled. He was quiet for a moment and then inhaled a deep breath and soldiered on. "As I said, this girl was totally naked, and she was passed out too. I checked to see if I could wake either of them up, and I couldn't. That's when I figured things were far more out of control than I'd understood at first. It wasn't until that minute that I actually figured out Pike had been roofied. I swear, I just thought he was comin' down with the flu or somethin'. But when that girl appeared…well, I finally pulled my head out of my butt and called 911. The 911 operator had me continue to try and wake up Pike and the girl until the paramedics arrived. I never was able to wake either one of them. They loaded Pike and the girl into two separate ambulances and hauled them off to the hospital." Again Charlie paused. "I almost got him killed over a damn fraternity pledge," he growled.

"Quit blamin' yourself, Charles," Harmony whispered, kissing Charlie on the head.

"And…and at the hospital? Did they find out what had been in Pike's drink?" Ambria urged—even though the story was making her feel like she might vomit herself.

Charlie nodded. "Yep. It really was Rohypnol," he answered. "Somebody roofied Pike with a big dose. And when he finally woke up…he didn't remember a thing. He didn't even remember goin' up the stairs with me, gettin' undressed, nothin'. And he sure as hell didn't remember Rayanne Bishop—although I know he'll never forget her now…not in all his life."

"Rayanne Bishop," Ambria stated. "The mysterious naked girl?"

Charlie nodded. "Rayanne Bishop," Charlie sighed. "We actually started callin' her Billie Jean after a time—you know, because of the pretense of the Michael Jackson song. We started callin' her that after a deputy sheriff showed up three months later with a warrant to collect Pike's DNA and tellin' him he was bein' accused of rape and…and fatherin' the baby Rayanne Bishop was carryin'."

"What?" Ambria gasped. It was worse than she'd even imagined it would be. "What? But…but he was passed out cold! You said he was passed out cold and so was she! How could he have...have done anything?"

"He couldn't have," Charlie affirmed. "But Rayanne found out she was pregnant, and since the timeline matched and she couldn't remember what had happened that night...she figured it was Pike. And she blamed him...claimed he roofied and raped her."

"But he couldn't have," Ambria repeated. Her thoughts ricocheted around in her brain, and she asked, "You were there! You were with him the whole time. Wasn't that enough to clear away any doubt?"

But Charlie shook his head. "Nope, it wasn't."

"Well, why not?" Harmony asked then. "You were a witness to what had happened to Pike and that he was passed out."

"Not for the three or four minutes I was in the bathroom," Charlie reminded. "And I think I got a little of whatever was goin' around too...'cause it took me too long to figure out somethin' was wrong with Pike, somethin' more than the flu. And those three or four minutes...Rayanne's attorney said I couldn't be sure it was only three or four minutes, not if I had drugs in me too."

"Oh, come on! Pike was out cold! How could he have possibly done anything to her?" Ambria asked again.

Charlie shrugged. "Well, Rayanne Bishop's attorney claimed that it could've happened easy in the time I was in the bathroom, that maybe Pike was fakin' that he was out cold...or even that he did the deed and then roofied himself to try and cover his tracks."

It was all so inconceivable—ridiculous! Yet Ambria knew that in this day and age, false accusations were a dime a dozen, especially if someone didn't want to face the truth. All at once, one of the Big Ten echoed in her mind—*Thou shalt not bear false witness against thy neighbor*—and she was further sickened by what a lot of people would do to keep themselves out of trouble. They'd throw anybody under the bus.

Still silent in astonished disbelief that Charlie's witness testimony hadn't been enough to stop the ridiculousness, Ambria asked, "But…but…but didn't they check her in the hospital? Once the paramedics got her to the hospital that night? Didn't they check her for…for whether or not she had…she had been intimate with anyone? Someone else's DNA was surely present."

But Charlie shook his head. "Nope. They didn't check her. They were too focused on makin' sure she recovered from bein' drugged. And anyway, Rayanne claimed she didn't even know she'd been intimate—or, as she claimed, sexually assaulted—until she discovered she was pregnant."

"Okay, but wait a minute," Ambria began, shaking her head as she tried to remember everything she knew about the law. "So she accused Pike, and they served a search warrant to collect his DNA. Paternity can be determined in, like, forty-eight hours these days. So? He gave a DNA sample, right?"

"He did," Charlie affirmed.

"So…wasn't he cleared almost right away?"

Charlie shook his head. "Nope. Not until six months later."

"Six months?" Harmony asked, frowning. "What took so long?"

"Well, this was six years ago," Charlie explained. "They have different types of tests available now, but back then they had to draw amniotic fluid while a woman was still pregnant if she wanted to determine paternity before her baby was born. And as you may or may not know—"

"There's a risk that that can cause a miscarriage," Ambria finished for him, exhaling a heavy sigh.

"Yep," Charlie confirmed. "Understandably, Rayanne Bishop didn't want to jeopardize her baby, so they collected Pike's blood, sent it off to the DNA lab…and then we all waited a long, long, long six months until Billie Jean's—I mean, Rayanne's—baby was born. Forty-eight hours after she had the baby, the results came back, provin' that Pike was not the father of Rayanne 'Billie Jean' Bishop's son. But the damage to Pike had already been done— emotionally, personally, financially, and of course reputation-wise. 'Cause for those six months before Rayanne Bishop gave birth, Pike got hate mail; he had people who recognized him from the newspaper articles about it, cussed at him in public, threw things at him…even had a restaurant that refused to serve him one time. Not to mention all the doubt the whole mess put in the minds of his friends and relatives. It was pure hell on him."

Ambria wiped tears from her cheeks. It was an inconceivable story—an inconceivably horrible thing to live through. And her heart ached for Pike.

"To her defense," Charlie continued, "and this is the only good thing I'll ever say about her, Rayanne Bishop did issue a public apology for falsely accusin' Pike…but it didn't help anything, really. The damage had already been done. And right after it was proven that Pike was not the father of her baby, everyone's attention moved on to poor Rayanne Bishop, who now had this baby from a 'date rape' situation and no memory of what happened. I mean, Pike actually felt sorry for her. I guess I did too, a little. But she could've waited until the baby was born to have Pike accused. If she'd waited, he would've gladly submitted to a DNA test at that time. But she didn't. Instead she drug his name through the mud, and his emotions and his life along with it."

"My heck," Harmony breathed. "How horrible for Pike. How horrible!"

"Anyway, that's what happened, Ambria," Charlie sighed. Frowning he added, "And your damn sister should've Googled Pike's name a little further than she did. He doesn't deserve to have this all stirred up again. I know it'll chew him up inside."

Ambria frowned too. "My sister," she grumbled, as anger began to well in her again. "She's…she's jealous. I know that's why she's done this to him…although she meant it to be done to me." As tears of anger began to spill over her cheeks, Ambria added, "And how selfish of her to do this to you two! Madison had to know this would cause so much misery for y'all as well. Oh, sometimes I just…I just loathe my sister!"

"Oh, we're fine, Ambria," Charlie assured her. "Nothin's goin' to ruin our weddin', now is it, baby?" He forced a rather sad grin, leaned over, and kissed Harmony on the mouth.

"No, sirree," Harmony agreed. "Nothin'! Especially not Madison."

"But…but what about Pike?" Ambria ventured. "He'll…he'll hate me for what Madison has done to him."

"No, no, no," Charlie interrupted. "Oh, believe me, he'll hate Madison for it…but not you." Charlie arched his eyebrows warily. "Although he might be worried that you'll change your mind about him or change how you feel about him because of all this…his past, so to speak."

Ambria leapt to her feet then. "His past? He doesn't have a past! He's been a victim of a crime, and of gossip and false accusation, but he's just as wonderful to me as he was before I heard any of this, and I love him just as much! More even!"

With intense determination rising in her bosom, Ambria asked, "Where would he go, Charlie? To calm down, to process it all? Where would he go? I've got to find him!"

Charlie shrugged. "Normally, for a drive or a walk. But he's dressed up like Vanilla Ice converted to male strippin'…so I don't know, 'cause his car is still here. I checked."

"I have to find him," Ambria wept. "I just have to find him! He has to know that I'm sorry for what happened to him, for Madison dredgin' it all up again! I just have to find him!"

"He'll be back, Ambria," Charlie assured her. "Pike won't stay away long, especially from you. He'll be back."

But Ambria didn't want to wait for Pike to cool off and come back, for him to process his pain and anger alone. She wanted to be with him as he processed it—hold him and kiss him and reassure him that it was all in the past.

"I'm goin' to find him," she stated. Nodding to Charlie, she said, "Thank you, Charlie, for tellin' me all this. I know it wasn't easy for you. And I also know you should quit blamin' yourself for it. It wasn't your fault."

She leaned over, planting a quick kiss of thanks to the top of Charlie's head. Sharing a quick hug with Harmony, Ambria said, "I'm goin' to find him."

"You go, girl," Harmony encouraged. "It's high time the man learned he doesn't have to deal with it on his own anymore."

With a nod, Ambria slipped on her sandals and hurried out of the room to search for Pike. "I'll find him," she whispered to herself, trying to ignore the quiet, nagging doubt in the back of her mind. "I will find him."

CHAPTER EIGHT

As Ambria left her bedroom—left Charlie and Harmony to some much-needed privacy—Kayla was heading toward the room she was sharing with Brooke.

"How are you, Ambria?" Kayla asked, an expression of sincere concern on her face. "I don't know what she said to you, but it appeared to me that your sister upset you…again. Are you all right?"

"Yes," Ambria assured her—even though, in truth, she wasn't yet certain she would be all right. "It's just one of the basic Madison nightmares."

"Well, I could see she upset Pike too, and he must not be over it yet because he's sittin' out there near the pool, kind of tucked back in the dark there by the laurel hedges," Kayla explained. Kayla shook her head. "That Madison! I do not know how you put up with her, Am. You're a better woman than I am."

Kayla hugged Ambria, and her friend's support did help to lift her heavy heart.

"Well, I hope you can keep whatever Madison did from eatin' at you too long, Am," Kayla offered. "I want you to be able to enjoy Harmony's weddin', you know?"

135

Ambria nodded. "I know…and I will," she promised. Little did Kayla know that, having innocently found where Pike had gone, she'd already helped Ambria more than she could ever understand.

"All right," Kayla sighed then. "Good night. I'm turnin' in, 'cause I'm as worn out as a three-legged work horse."

"Good night, Kayla…and thank you," Ambria called as Kayla headed toward her room.

Ambria paused for a moment—for although her instinct and desire were to race out to the laurel hedges near the pool, throw herself into Pike's arms, and weep with her own heartache at what he had endured, she knew that he needed more than just her empathy-induced weeping and reassurance. Pike obviously possessed a very strong, resilient character. Many people would've let an incident like the one he had endured determine who they were from then on. But not Pike. He'd risen above it; he owned a deep emotional scar that would never completely leave him, but it hadn't become who he was. Pike was so strong—stronger than Ambria had even realized. Furthermore, though she had always recognized the strength he had encouraged in her four years before, in those moments she was also aware of the strength she'd found in herself over the last week because of him. Never, not in all her life, had she stood up to Madison the way she had that night. Although Ambria had grown better and better at not allowing Madison to drag down her self-confidence and at not being bullied, this was different. This time, Ambria's heart and soul had known a strength they never had before, and it was Pike who helped it to begin to resonate through her entire being. Over less than a week, he had added to her own strength of character.

Therefore, having paused before racing off to throw herself into Pike's embrace, Ambria's mind had settled a bit—and she knew

136

what would serve Pike better that night. Rehashing the painful event in his past had most likely been something he'd done over and over and over again. Even that night she knew he had—knew that once his anger toward Madison had subsided a bit, the memories of the whole Rayanne Bishop mess would've washed over him like sickening, unwelcome swamp water. There would be plenty of time for him to tell the story to her in his own way. But tonight—tonight he needed distraction, he needed reassurance through action, he needed to be loved.

Hurrying back to her bedroom, Ambria quickly explained that Kayla had sighted Pike out by the pool and how she planned to help him. Changing into the blue sequined bathing suit that Harmony had gifted her, Ambria then raced to Charlie and Pike's room to retrieve Pike's board shorts.

"Yep," she mumbled to herself as she dashed into the bathroom of Charlie and Pike's room to find Pike's board shorts hanging on a hook on the back of the bathroom door just where Charlie said they would be.

Then, hesitating in order to inhale and exhale deeply to calm herself a little, Ambria walked out onto the back patio.

As she laid Pike's board shorts on a patio chair someone had left at the pool's edge, she called, "Wanna go for a swim?"

There was silence at first, but after a time Pike responded from the shadows, asking, "Are you talkin' to me?"

"If you're Pike O'Leary, the Vanilla Ice stripper boy, then yes," she answered.

"What if I'm a date-rapin', dead-beat dad?" he growled with residual anger, not self-pity.

"You're not, and I want to be with you in the pool right now," Ambria said, removing her sarong and tossing it onto the chair next to Pike's board shorts. "We can talk about all that mess another time. Charlie gave me the gist of it, and I'd already figured it was somethin' like that anyway, so we'll have plenty of time to go over it when you feel more like it. But right now, I just want to be alone with you again. This was a very demandin' night for me socially, and my purse is completely empty."

"Your what?" Pike asked, still lingering in the shadows.

"My purse," she said as she slowly descended the graduated steps leading into the pool. "It's an analogy my daddy told me years ago. Some people love parties and socializin'; they draw energy from it, feel revitalized by it. Those are the extroverts in the world. Bein' social fills an extrovert's empty purse, meanin' it fills them up with energy. But me and my daddy, we're introverts. Our purses are full when we're alone, and then socializin' empties them out. I gain my energy by bein' in a quiet place alone or with someone I love. So you see, after this party tonight—after dealin' with my older sister's malice again, after knowin' what you went through years ago and my heart achin' for you—my purse is plum empty. So I need some time alone with you...you know, so you can refill my purse like my daddy explained to me."

"Your daddy is a wise man," Pike said, slowing striding from the shadows to stand next to the pool.

Ambria's heart skipped several beats as she stared up at the tall, gorgeous drink of water standing at the edge of the pool looking down at her. "Hi there," she said softly. "You wanna join me? I brought your suit out with me."

Pike grinned, even for the fatigue that was evident in his eyes. "You did, huh?" he asked, hunkering down and seeming to check the temperature of the water with his fingers.

"Yes, I did," Ambria affirmed.

She watched as Pike stood straight once more and then doubled over to remove the black shoes and socks he was wearing, haphazardly tossing them over his shoulder. Ambria smiled as she watched them scatter here and there among the laurel hedge behind him.

"Well, I'm glad you thought ahead," Pike O'Leary, the most gorgeous, beefcaked, super-stud lady-killer Ambria had ever seen in all her life said as a grin curved his alluring lips. "But I don't see the need for them."

Ambria gasp-giggled as Pike then quickly stripped off his MC Hammer harem-style pants, tossing them over his shoulder as well.

"I'm wearing my boxer briefs, and that's all I need," he said before jumping into the pool and making his way toward her. Ambria giggled as he took her in his arms and began leading them into the deeper water. She knew she'd never forget the sight of him putting every Calvin Klein male underwear model to shame with his perfect physique and black boxer briefs a moment before joining her in the pool.

As Ambria started to put her arms around his neck, she paused, smiling and informing him, "You forgot somethin'."

"What's that?" he asked as he placed a tender kiss to her neck.

"You don't need this anymore either," she answered, taking hold of the black bow tie he still wore on a black, Velcro-fastened ribbon around his neck. Pulling it off, she quickly tossed it back over her shoulder to land on the patio behind her.

Pike gazed at her for a long time, silently studying her. "Ambria..." he began. "I'm sorry I didn't tell you about it all before—"

"Shhh," Ambria soothed, pressing her fingertips to his mouth to lovingly hush him. "Do you want to talk about it right now, Pike?

If you do, I'm here, and I'm listenin', and I want to listen. But…if you've had enough of it for tonight, Charlie told me the story…and we can wait until another time. Either way, I want to do what's best for you right now."

Pike frowned a little, but for only an instant before replying, "I want to push it away for tonight, if you don't mind, baby. I've spent a lot of time boilin' over about it, and if…if you understand and don't think badly of me because of…because of Charlie's explanation, then I'd rather just hold you in my arms, pull you around the pool, listen to the bugs gettin' caught up in the rapture of the bug zapper, and look forward to the future right now."

Ambria smiled, relieved that her intuition had led her to react to Pike the way he needed her to that night.

"Then let's do just that," she whispered, slipping her arms around his neck. "Let's just relax, enjoy one another, and look to the future. After all, our best friends are gettin' married day after tomorrow, and that's a happy thing to look forward to."

"And as for your sister—" Pike began.

"Shhh," Ambria shushed, placing a kiss to his lips so he couldn't talk. "I don't want to talk about the M-word tonight either. I just want to be with you right now."

Ambria gazed up into the blue, blue, blue of Pike's eyes. Even the blue sequins on her bathing suit couldn't hold a candle to their brilliance—their sudden emotion.

"You make me a better man, Miss Blanchard," he mumbled. "I'm a far better man today than I was before last weekend when I walked into Mancini's and saw you there. I was a better man four years ago after I had supper with your family and met you."

"You've got me where you want me, Mr. O'Leary," Ambria teased. "No need to flatter me any further to draw me in closer to—"

"But I'm serious, Ambria," he assured her, frowning a little. "You make me better. You make me myself."

Ambria felt warm tears welling in her eyes. "You make me myself too, Pike," she confessed. "You make me brave, value who I am, and see that I am a good person…and that I shouldn't let others try to cause me to think anything else."

Pike kissed her softly, tenderly.

"Then maybe my daddy is wise like yours," he said in the low, alluring voice that always caused Ambria's knees to weaken. "Because whenever this nightmare comes up, he tells me that one day, when I'm fifty or so, I'll look back on it all, realize how asinine it all was, and probably even laugh a little. Although it's hard for me to imagine that now."

Ambria reached up, caressing his strong, whiskery jaw. "I think he's right. You might even find you don't hate the Michael Jackson song 'Billie Jean' as much as I'm sure you do now."

Again Pike grinned. "Charlie told you about that, huh?"

"He did," Ambria confirmed.

"Did he tell you about the celebrity impersonation I perfected at that time, as well?"

"No," Ambria giggled. "Celebrity impersonation?"

Pointing one index finger at Ambria and tipping his head to one side, Pike then produced a perfect impersonation of President Bill Clinton, saying, "I did not have sex'al relations with that woman."

As serious as the matter had been, and still was, Ambria couldn't keep from laughing—for Pike's impersonation was spot on! His mannerisms, his gesture, his perfected Arkansas accent, and of course his verbiage were perfect—a perfect impersonation of Bill Clinton and his statement of January 28, 1998, denying his romantic involvement with then-White House intern Monica Lewinsky.

"I'm sorry! I know I shouldn't laugh, but that is perfect, Pike. Perfect!" Ambria giggled.

Pike's smile finally broadened to indicate he was moving beyond the pain Madison had inflicted on him that night. "You want to hear it again?" he chuckled as Ambria wiped tears of mirth from her eyes.

"Yes!" she assured him through her laughter.

Again, Pike leveled an index finger, waving it pointedly as he said, "I did not have sex'al relations with that woman."

Ambria laughed even harder this time—laughed not only because Pike's impersonation was so flawless but also with a lightened heart in knowing he could still deal with the negative emotions the nightmare had caused through humor.

"I didn't, you know," Pike said quietly, as if he felt he needed to reiterate the truth to Ambria—the truth she already knew was truth.

"I know, Vanilla…I know," she said, staring into his blue-blue-blues so he could see her sincerity.

"Vanilla?" he inquired, quirking one handsome brow.

"Vanilla Ice," she reminded him. Smiling and weaving her hands through his hair at the back of his neck, she said. "I never imagined that the man of my dreams would turn out to have the heart of Mr. Rogers, the moves of Vanilla Ice, and the voice of Bill Clinton."

Understanding her teasing then, Pike again leveled his index finger at her, starting, "I did not have—"

But Ambria again gently hushed him with her fingertips. "Um, I like your voice so much better, by the way. You can keep Mr. Rogers' heart and Vanilla Ice's moves…but I always want to hear your deep, sexy voice and not Bill Clinton's, okay? Promise?"

"I do," Pike chuckled.

Wrapping his arms tightly around Ambria's waist then and slowly moving them into deeper water, Pike kissed Ambria's cheek, her neck, her shoulder. And once they were in deep enough water that her feet couldn't touch the bottom of the pool and she had to cling to him to stay above the surface, he said, "You wanna make out?"

Ambria smiled as her heart leapt inside her—as the butterflies in her stomach catapulted into activity. "I do," she answered in a whisper.

It was pure passion between them then—a melding of hearts— a mingling of mouths—sublime affections of two souls that were attuned.

"Well, that worked out a lot quicker than I expected," Charlie said as he and Harmony peered out through a small window in the entertainment room to the goings-on between Pike and Ambria in the pool.

Harmony smiled, sighing with contentment. "It's because Ambria's so able to read any situation and do what's most needed." She turned to Charlie then, taking his face between her hands and kissing him square on the mouth. "Thank you, darlin'! Thank you!"

"For what?" Charlie asked, puzzled.

"For bringin' Pike back to Ambria after all these years," Harmony answered.

Charlie frowned. "What do you mean, after all these years?"

But Harmony shook her head, giggling. "Never mind, Vanilla Ice. Never mind."

With that, Charlie began to beatbox the opening measures to "Ice Ice Baby" as he took hold of Harmony's waist and began to swivel his hips. Harmony laughed as he began to "sing" the song and continued to dance.

"Oh, you dork," she giggled, pulling Charlie into her arms and behind the blackout curtains that led to the theater room. "You stop that and give me some Vanilla Ice sugar, husband-to-be."

"Your wish is my command, wife-to-be," Charlie said as he captured Harmony's mouth in an impassioned kiss of true, lasting, forevermore love.

Harmony's heart was light and happy, for not only was she in love with Charlie—not only was he more than she ever dreamed a man could be—but she also knew Pike would be to her adored friend Ambria just what Charlie was to her—everything!

EPILOGUE

Tears of joy welled in Ambria's eyes as she watched Harmony walk down the aisle toward Charlie as Harmony's aunts—professional opera singers—flawlessly sang "The Flower Duet" from the opera *Lakmé*. As she watched Harmony's little three-year-old cousin scattering rose petals on the red carpet before Harmony, Ambria was sure she would never see or hear anything so beautiful in all her life. There stood Charlie, eyes moist with emotion, love, and admiration for the beautiful young woman slowly making her way to him. Dressed in her white, ethereally exquisite mermaid bridal gown, her soft sable hair swept up into the most perfect coiffure and embellished with three gardenias, Harmony was the archetypal bride.

Struggling to keep her tears of happiness from spilling out of her eyes and over her cheeks, Ambria looked away from Harmony and across the wedding riser to where Pike stood next to Charlie. The other groomsmen stood in a line beside him, just as the other bridesmaids stood in a line beside Ambria.

The moment Ambria looked to Pike, her heart began to beat with such vigor inside her that she could peripherally see the long banana curl caressing the right side of her face begin to tremble. Pike was so very handsome! Each time Ambria looked at him, she stood in awed disbelief for a moment at how attractive and alluring he really was. Dressed in the slick navy suit and tie Harmony had chosen for Charlie's groomsmen, Pike also wore the shell-pink shirt that matched her own shell-pink mermaid gown. Her smile broadened as she remembered the conversation she and Pike had had only an hour before.

"I can't believe she's got me and Charlie in pink," Pike had grumbled.

"Oh, now hush," Ambria had teased. "You know shell pink is your best color."

Pike had rolled his eyes, noting, "I'd feel a little better if you called it conch-shell pink instead of just shell pink. At least conch-shell pink sounds…sounds…"

"Heavier? More masculine?" she offered.

"Yeah," Pike had affirmed. "After all, conch shells are the badasses of the shell community—or so I've been told—even if they do have pink on them."

"Okay then," Ambria giggled. "Your shirt is conch-shell pink…if that makes you feel more manly."

"It does," Pike assured her.

As Harmony stepped up onto the riser to stand facing Charlie, Ambria almost giggled out loud at the memory of Pike's stating that conch shells were "the badasses of the shell community." But she didn't. Instead, as the pastor began the wedding ceremony, she turned so that her stance was in line with Harmony's as the bride faced the groom. But even as the ceremony proceeded, Ambria couldn't keep from glancing to Pike. And every time she did glance at him, or allowed her gaze to linger on him, he was staring directly at her—not paying attention at all to the ceremony.

In fact, Pike was staring at Ambria with such perpetual focus that at last she risked mouthing, *What?* to him—for she was certain her dress must be falling off or something. Why else would he be staring at her so intently?

Ever since she and Harmony had performed in the school talent show when they were in first grade, Ambria had been paranoid that her dress was going to fall off—and for good reason. Ambria and Harmony had signed up to perform their newest dance recital routine in the school talent show. After all, they'd worked very hard on learning the steps their dance teacher had taught them, choreography to "The Glow-Worm," painstakingly practicing for months. They even had costumes! The dance class had worn lovely sky-blue tutus that tied at the back of their necks and were embellished with silver sequins. At six years old, to them their tutus were the equivalent of prom dresses to high school girls.

And so they had signed up for the school talent show, and when the day came that they were to perform—well, disaster had struck, a disaster that would haunt Ambria forever, even if it were Harmony who should have been haunted. Approximately halfway through their dance routine, Ambria (her hands placed firmly on her hips per the choreography) glanced over to Harmony to see how she was doing. It was the very first time in her life that Ambria had been truly and excruciatingly embarrassed. Somehow the ribbon ties at the top of the tutu, which tied at the back of the neck and anchored Harmony's tutu bodice, had untied, and as Ambria watched in helpless horror, Harmony's tutu top began to slide down. And then, all at horrifically once, Harmony's entire tutu bodice flopped over onto her belly, leaving Harmony buck-naked from the waist up. To that very day, Ambria couldn't remember how the situation had ended. Had Harmony's mom rushed in from the stage wings to save her daughter's modesty? Had the dance been close enough to coming at an end that Harmony had raced off the stage? Ambria couldn't remember. And although Ambria's mother remembered and assured Ambria that Harmony's mom had paused the CD, raced out onto the stage, and resecured Harmony's tutu top, and that she and Harmony had then finished their dance routine, Ambria couldn't remember it all. Therefore, Ambria had been left with a lifelong fear that some dress she was wearing might someday fall off when she was in public.

What? she mouthed to Pike again.

But his smile only broadened, and he mouthed, *Look down.*

Thinking her worst fear was about to be realized and that she would look down to see her dress had slipped off, revealing her chest—her bosoms—Ambria looked down. Thankfully, she found that her dress was still fine.

What? she mouthed at Pike again, attempting not to distract anyone from the ongoing wedding ceremony between Harmony and Charlie.

Look at your flowers, Pike mouthed to her then.

Why? Ambria asked. The thought popped into her mind that maybe there was a big spider crawling out of her bouquet, a horrifying thought in itself. Ambria still did not want to distract from the ceremony. Slowly she looked down at her pretty bouquet of pink peonies and white gardenias. When she didn't see a spider emerging anywhere, she began to exhale a sigh of relief. However, as her gaze fell to something else, tears filled her eyes. This time the tears were for her own joy, and she could not keep them from escaping her eyes to trickle over her cheeks—for there, in the center of her maid-of-honor bouquet, perched perfectly on a small clear plastic flower pick, was the most beautiful solitaire engagement ring she had ever seen!

Breathless with disbelief, Ambria looked up to Pike again. He was still smiling, gazing at her with his blue, blue, bluest eyes as he mouthed, *Will you marry me?*

In truth, Ambria was sure she might faint! How could she possibly keep her balance when her mind and heart were so awhirl?

Yet without hesitation and managing not to faint, she mouthed, *Yes*, to Pike. Instantly moisture rose in his eyes, and when he winked at her, one lone tear traveled down his right cheek.

"What're you doin', baby?" Pike asked as he stepped into the pool and sat down next to her on one of the lower graduated steps that led down into the water. Ambria grinned as she watched him take the cinnamon toothpick from his mouth and set it on the tile at the pool's edge.

"Just rememberin' where we were last year at this time," she told him.

Turning to look at him, Pike reached out, brushing a tear from her cheek.

"Oh, don't cry, darlin'," he said, gathering her into his arms. Chuckling, he lovingly asked, "How long are you goin' to get all mushy over that?" He kissed the top of her head.

"Probably forever," Ambria admitted.

Gazing down at her with the blue, blue, bluest eyes Ambria had still ever seen, Pike said, "Me too, actually."

"I'm glad," Ambria whispered, kissing his neck.

"And I'm glad Madison agreed to put the ring in your bouquet for me," Pike added. "It helped me, you know…helped me…"

"To not hate her anymore?" Ambria offered with a smile.

"Yep," Pike admitted. "Now I can be happy for her gettin' married to Alvin next month. If she hadn't done that, I might have warned him to head for the hills when they first started datin'."

Standing, Pike pulled Ambria into the water and against the strength of his body. As he pulled her into the deeper water, he kissed her—kissed her a kiss that had become so familiar and so very beloved to her over the past year. If nothing else in all the world were true, Pike O'Leary's kisses were delicious in their satisfying, seductive quality. His kiss was always euphoric to Ambria, and she knew it always would be.

"Hey!" Charlie called from his place at the grill on the patio. "Don't you go makin' babies in our pool, you two. These burgers are almost finished."

"Oh, we won't," Pike called from the pool. Gazing into Ambria's eyes, he smiled and whispered, "Our baby is already made, isn't that right?"

"Yes, it is," Ambria giggled.

"At least our first one, anyway," Pike added. "Can I tell Charlie today?"

"Of course," Ambria assured him. "But let me tell Harm first, okay?"

"Anything you want, baby," Pike agreed.

"I'm so glad you made your potato salad, Am," Harmony called as she set the large bowl of potato salad on the patio table. "Next to your red stuff and noodles, this is my favorite thing that you make!"

And although Ambria heard her friend, she didn't speak to respond—for she was too enchanted by the love she could see in her husband's eyes.

"I love you," she whispered.

"I love you," Pike mumbled in return.

And as his cinnamon-flavored mouth continued to prove to Ambria that he loved her with kisses that made her heart race, her knees weak, and her toes curl, Pike began to hum "It's You I Like." In the next moment, he broke the seal of their kiss and began to sing it to her—and as he did, she joined him in singing the song a quiet, wise icon of the last century wrote to encourage acceptance and love.

"Hold up," Charlie said to Harmony, frowning. "Are they...they're not singin' a Mr. Rogers' song, are they?"

Harmony smiled, her heart full of joy for herself as well as for Ambria—for both she and her best friend had found true and enduring forever love.

"Yep. They are. It's their song, you know—that 'It's You I Like' song by Mr. Rogers," Harmony explained.

Charlie quirked one astonished eyebrow. "And I thought it was weird that 'Ice Ice Baby' was our song."

"There goes Charlie," Pike chuckled as he pulled Ambria around the pool. "Ice Ice'n his woman again."

Ambria glanced over to where Charlie was swiveling his hips as he danced around Harmony, singing Vanilla Ice's iconic song. "They're so funny!"

"Hey, hold up!" Charlie called all of a sudden. Hurrying over to where his phone was docked, he fiddled with it for a moment. A moment later, "Ice Ice Baby" began to play, and Charlie put down his grilling fork and began to really bust loose.

"Come on, Pike!" he called. "Let's see if we can still get these women's hearts to poundin' with our sexiness."

Applying one last commanding, hungry kiss to Ambria's mouth as he moved her into shallow water, Ambria watched Pike lift himself out of the pool and hurry to join Charlie in dancing.

Ambria watched Pike dance for a moment, admiring his perfect body, thinking for the billionth time that he was the most gorgeous, beefcaked, super-stud lady-killer she had ever seen and suddenly overwhelmed with the love they shared. After a time she glanced to Harmony to find her friend staring at her with mutually shared happiness.

"Come on, baby," Pike called to Ambria. "Get out here and shake that little mermaid fanny of yours for me!"

Laughing, Ambria hurried out of the pool to join him. In an instant, the two couples were dancing and singing together without any inhibitions. As Pike took Ambria in his arms again, she remembered who she had been before he'd entered her life: a self-conscious, often self-loathing, target for Madison and others. But not now—not now. Pike O'Leary loved her! Pike O'Leary had chosen her over any other woman in all the world. And in that alone, regardless of everything else she'd learned—everything else Pike had gifted her—that alone was proof that she really was special.

"Kiss me, you gorgeous, beefcaked super-stud of mine!" Ambria playfully demanded, reaching up to take Pike's handsome face between her hands.

"You don't have to tell me twice, woman," Pike growled seductively as he ground an impassioned kiss to Ambria's mouth. And as her toes curled, her knees weakened, and the butterflies in her stomach took flight, Ambria O'Leary thanked heaven for the fact that her older sister had once tried to reel in a man far and away too good for her—thanked heaven Pike had snapped Madison's line. For he was the perfect catch—the perfect catch and meant for

Ambria. As Pike continued to thrill her with his sumptuous, sublime kisses, Ambria thanked heaven he had landed in her purse, and would fill her purse, forevermore.

AUTHOR'S NOTE

None of us get through life unscathed—neither physically nor emotionally. I'm scathed, you're scathed, we're all scathed. And unfortunately, one of the most emotionally detrimental, scarring things we all endure often revolves around some physical attribute we possess. I know people who were teased about their feet when they were young, and for the rest of their lives they are self-conscious about their feet, even resenting the fact that they don't have gorgeous feet. I have friends who have been teased about the size or shape of their noses, their hands, and their freckles. One friend was posing for her senior portraits, and the photographer said, "Smile!" She did smile. "Oh, honey! That's terrible!" the photographer told her. "You look like a horse. Too gummy. Tone it down, okay?" And yes, for the rest of her life, she was self-conscious about her smile. I've known guys who were teased because they were too skinny, too fat, not muscular enough, on and on. I have girlfriends who were teased because they were "flat as a pancake" in the bosom region. My point is, because of someone's thoughtlessness, teasing, or cruelty, we all have something we're dissatisfied about concerning our physical appearance. And as you've guessed by now, my biggest albatross in that area—yep, my boobs!

You see, I started wearing a bra in the fourth grade. By age eleven and in sixth grade, I was five-foot-four (never grew another inch in height) and was wearing a 34C bra. Furthermore, unlike the way things are today—where a lot of young girls are impatient to develop, to begin wearing bras—I was a weirdo back then! Not only did I have the body of a sixteen-to-twenty-year-old, I was unique and stuck out like a sore thumb. From the tender age of nine, I began enduring lewd remarks and propositions from boys—being grabbed, groped, teased. Girls were mean too, making fun of me for being such a "freak of nature." Therefore, I began hating my body, specifically my boobs, very early on. If it hadn't been for my friend Amy L.C.L., who had a very similar body shape and bra size, I don't know what I would've done. Still, she went to a different elementary and middle school than I did, so I was at the mercy of meanies every weekday of every week for years.

Of course, as I matured emotionally, as well as reached an age where I wasn't the weirdo in every group of girls, I handled the fact that my bazoombas were "above average in size" better than I had as a kid. But I still had to volley the lewd remarks, the staring—now not only from boys but also from men—and the odd attempts guys made to brush against me or outright "cop a feel." (Yeah, *cop a feel* is an ugly phrase. But I use it because that's how I still feel about boys and men who tried to do it.) That, and the overwhelming fact that the world at that time made me feel like I was dressing immodestly just because I had a figure, caused me and still causes me to want to hide in my clothes. As a young adolescent, I felt like I had done something wrong or that there was something wrong with me—or at least my body. I felt like I had a "bad" body—and not in the way *bad* meant *good* in the '80s. Self-conscious and with a growing attitude that all males of the species were perverts, I really have never stopped hating my boobs. Now, admittedly, this is something that my husband just couldn't wrap his mind around for a long time, especially when we were first married. I mean, when we got married, my body measurements were 36-inch bust, 19-inch waist, and 35-inch hips—Rachel Welch's measurements at the height of her fame (only with a smaller waist)—and I hated my body! One day, Kevin (my husband) realized that the way he felt when he was a kid and teen when people would make fun of him and call him "skinny" was exactly how I felt about my boobs. That's when he got it; that's what made him empathize with my feelings. Please don't misunderstand. I certainly had other body issues too— self-conscious feelings about other things spurred by negative things people had said to me when I was a child and teenager. But nothing outweighed my boob-resentment.

You might be asking, "Why is she going on and on and endlessly on about her boob-loathing?" Well, I'll tell you: because I know that every one of us (especially women) hides some sort of self-loathing about something in our physical appearance. It may be a nose, ears, eyes, freckles, lips, smile, teeth, feet, knees, elbows, wrists, chubbiness, skinniness, big boobs, little boobs—but we all have something. Sure, we're thankful that we're alive and have a body that works well; there are those who have special needs physically that we don't have. But it's still difficult to process and deal with, especially as a child or teenager, and it sets the tone for what we see in the mirror looking back at us for the rest of our lives.

For those of you who are under the age of fifty, I will give you this hope: when you hit fifty or close to it, you get to a point where you just have the attitude of, "Screw you guys! I hate high school!" You are who you are, you're just grateful to be alive and in good health, and you're able to quit obsessing over and resenting the physical traits that you deem imperfect, or that someone else made you feel is imperfect. I still resent my boobs a lot these days, but that being said, now I find that I resent them more because when I lay flat on my back in bed, they migrate up toward my throat and nearly choke me to death!

My point to all this rambling on is this: I want us all to be conscious of the fact that 99.9 percent of we human beings struggle with some sort of disappointing physical attribute of ourselves, and most of the reason is because of something somebody said during our formative years. What would we have been like had people said only kind things to us about ourselves? I understand that emotional scarring is part of life, even necessary for our growth. After all, a scar isn't who you are; it's where you've been, what you've learned. And I think most of us are kind and don't say negative things to people about their appearance. But even teasing can harm the tender self-worth, self-image, and self-confidence of a person, no matter their age. In truth, I loathe teasing more than I loathe my boobs! I always tell my husband that there is "teasing down" and "teasing up." Teasing up would be something like, "Wow! I wish I had your hair! You could be a Disney princess with that hair." Whereas teasing down is something we are all too familiar with—something like, "Wow, I guess instead of skinny dipping you go chunky dunky, right?" If I had my choice, teasing down would get people flogged!

Ambria eventually came to deal with her rockin' bod. Pike even helped her see that it wasn't a bad thing to have it. I'm so grateful I *do* have a Pike in my life! Kevin counteracts all the bad boob stuff I went through before I married him. But not everyone has a Pike; not everyone has an Ambria either. How much personal agony could Ambria have avoided if her boobs hadn't been termed as freakish by her older sister? How much less misery would Pike have had to endure if people waited to pass judgment until they had been presented all the facts with what happened to him at the frat party?

I guess my personal point—and the reason I wrote this little romantic romp that included issues with big boobs and false accusations—is this. Don't do it. Don't be unkind—not at all! Don't tease down, and *never* make fun of someone's something. That kind of hurt scars, and those scars never really heal. We should never contribute to someone's insecurities about his or her appearance. Never. There's no good reason to say something that will make a person self-conscious about their smile, their nose, or their boobs for the rest of their life.

And now, after all that serious blah-blah, let's have some fun! Just to give you an idea of what I'm talking about, here is a photograph with the heads cropped off of me at age eleven standing with my aunt, who was thirty-four at the time. I'm sure you can tell which one is me, and although you *cannot* tell how big my boobs are from this snapshot, when you see the full photograph—when you see how preadolescent my face looks—you'll get it! So the no-heads boobs picture of me and my aunt—not that unusual, right?

But then…bam! Eleven years old with that rockin' bod? It was a nightmare! Ha ha ha!

As always, I hope you enjoyed *The Groomsman*—found it enjoyable and giggled a few times, even if my inspiration for certain parts of it wasn't as lighthearted as some might think. Furthermore, there *is* fun ahead! So many of you have written to me letting me know that you so enjoy the Author's Notes in my books that I've given you some extra-informative snippets this time, as well as two recipes! I hope you enjoy them. Thank you for living *The Groomsman* with me!

With Love,
Marcia Lynn McClure

Snippet #1—Red Stuff and Noodles. This really is one of our family's top three favorite meals; I would put it as number one overall. And the history of how it became red stuff and noodles is exactly as Erica describes it the prologue of this book! I've shared this before and had so many friends tell me it quickly became a favorite with their family too. And so, here it is—straight out of my personal cookbook computer file. I give you Red Stuff and Noodles!

Red Stuff and Noodles

Ingredients:

3 pounds stew meat or roast (tenderized and cut into bite-size pieces)

2 medium onions (coarsely chopped)

4 tablespoons butter

4 cups water

2 teaspoons garlic powder

1½ cups ketchup

4 tablespoons Worcestershire sauce

⅓ cup brown sugar

2 tablespoons mustard

½ teaspoon salt

4 teaspoons paprika

¼ teaspoon cayenne pepper

Extra-wide egg noodles

Melt butter in large electric skillet and brown meat over medium heat. Add onion and sauté until tender. Add remaining ingredients (except noodles) and cover. Simmer for 1 to 2 hours until meat is tender and sauce is thick.

Serve over hot noodles!

Note: I found the basis for this recipe in my cookbook when I was first married. I've made so many changes that I don't even remember the original recipe or what it was called. However, I do believe it was Sandy who started requesting "that red stuff with noodles." Thus, it's been known as "red stuff and noodles" ever since—at least to our little family. Red stuff and noodles is to my kids what Corn Flake chicken was to me and my sister—the favorite family main dish recipe!

Snippet #2—Hadley's lack of tact was based exclusively on some of the epic "tactless" antics of my little sister, Luanna. Although Hadley is older in the prologue than my sister was during her tactless catastrophes (Hadley being eleven and my sister between the ages of six to eight years old at the height of her tactlessness), I promise you, Luanna's shenanigans were even more hysterical than Hadley's!

When I begin thinking of Luanna's lack-of-tact incidents, three in particular leap to the forefront of my mind immediately.

One day in the foyer of our church building, a big bunch of people were standing around having a good time in conversation. There was a young man amid them who was nineteen or twenty years old and whose face was completely broken out in red, angry-looking pimples. Luanna walked up to him, frowning as she stared at him for a moment. Then, in a loud voice so that she was sure he could hear her over the noise of the other people's voices, she asked,

"What are those red spots all over your face?" Yep! She said it, and the guy's face turned as red as his poor pimples! Poor guy. But hey, Luanna was prepubescent and therefore had no experience with pimples. "I was just wondering," she told me afterward.

The second incident that is completely unforgettable happened in at the Coronado movie theater in Albuquerque. I wasn't quite sixteen, so that would've made Luanna about eight years old. I had taken Luanna and a couple of our friends to a movie. As we took our seats in the darkened theater, preparing to enjoy *Clash of the Titans* '80s style, Luanna noticed something about the lady sitting in front of us. The lady had an awesome 'fro going and, as was the style then, had her Afro pick tucked in her hair (for convenience and easy accessibility) with the handle showing (to look cool). Before I knew what was about to happen, Luanna leaned forward and tapped the lady on the shoulder. When the lady turned around to see what Luanna wanted, Luanna said, "Hey, lady...did you know you have a comb stuck in your hair?" True story—no kidding.

For my third and final (for now) cherished "Luanna had no tact filter yet" story, here we go. So, our family had invited the missionaries (Mormon missionaries) over for dinner one night. The young men were very nice and arrived early. In fact, they arrived so early that evening that they ended up sitting down in our living room as we finished watching a movie on TV. (The movie was either *The Sound of Music* or *The Ten Commandments*, but I can't remember which for certain.) We had turned out the lights in the house as to better enjoy the movie. Keep in mind, this was before people could record movies off TV and watch them later. That meant, that if we wanted to see the end of the movie, we had to watch it then and there. The missionaries were very understanding and plopped down in a couple of seats behind us. I remember Luanna sitting cross-legged there in front of the TV, the warm glow of the TV lights illuminating her face and giving her the appearance of a sweet, porcelain-cheeked cherub. Well, as it turned out, one of the missionaries was a severe asthmatic. He was wheezing very loudly, but we all knew that it was something the young man had to deal with in life. Sure, it was a bit distracting, but he couldn't help it, of course, and we all knew that. Well, my mom, my dad, the other missionary, and I all knew that. However, apparently Luanna did not. A few minutes after we started to watch the movie again, the missionaries along for the ride, Luanna sits straight up and frowning with profound irritation nearly shouted, "Who is breathing like a monster?" Now, to her defense, when I was talking to her today about this particular incident, she says she remembers that since we were all sitting in the dark, she thought someone was breathing like a monster on purpose to try and scare her. You know—because *The Sound of Music* is so scary, right?

And there you have it! My little sister's antics—perfect inspiration for Hadley's youthful tactlessness when Madison first brings Pike to supper.

Snippet #3—Several years ago, I was with a friend (whom we'll call Violet) for lunch, and we met one of her friends (let's name her Sybil) and her friend's fifteen-year-old daughter (we'll call her Sabrina). Sybil was a tall, very slender woman, very well dressed and very confident. Her daughter, Sabrina, was shorter, a very pretty girl with a killer bod! As you can imagine, I immediately felt a kindredness to Sabrina, knowing she had probably "developed" very young and was outranking her mom by leaps and bounds where body shape was concerned.

So we're all sitting there at lunch, and Violet (who was soon to be married) says something about the fact that her wedding dress wouldn't fit her bust line if she gained even one more pound before the wedding. All at once Sybil laughs.

"Speaking of big boobs, look at this freak!" Sybil cackled, pointing to he daughter. "Can you believe the size of Sabrina's boobs? What a rack! And she's only fifteen! What a freakin' freak!"

This is not a fictional story. This really happened. I woke up one night last year thinking about how horrible it was—that a mother would make fun of her daughter like that. A girl's body image is so fragile, at any age but especially in adolescence, and Sabrina's expression in that horrible moment is permanently etched in my mind. So there you have my inspiration for Ambria's sister Madison the Meany. And by the way, I made Madison the villain instead of Erica, because I couldn't fathom writing that Ambria's mother would be so cruel to her. Unbelievable, right?

Snippet #4—Chunk the dog. As I was writing the prologue of *The Groomsman*, I was struggling to find a name I liked for the Blanchards' beloved dog. Kevin and I own a Lab-Rhodesian ridgeback, 80-pound lapdog named Charlie. (Holy cow! I just now realized that Charlie Oaks—the groom—is named after our dog!) And although our Charlie was indeed the inspiration for the Blanchard family's dog (and obviously Harmony's groom, Charlie), I could not think of a name I liked for their dog. As fate would have it, and as it often does when I'm stuck on something important like this, Kevin was sauntering past my open office door.

"Hey!" I called. "What's a good name for a dog for my book? Maybe something out of one of our favorite movies."

Without even an instant of hesitation, Kevin said, "Chunk…from *The Goonies.*"

Eureka! I loved it! Thus, Chunk became Chunk! I kept seeing the Truffle Shuffle in my mind every time I wrote about the Blanchards' dog after that.

Snippet #5—Pike's canary-yellow Mustang. The story of Pike's canary-yellow Mustang is deeply rooted in our family's real-life history. In May 2007, our oldest son, Mitch, was finishing his junior year in high school. He'd been driving our little run-around car—a blue Dodge Neon stick shift. One day, as he was taking some friends to a movie, he and the Neon were T-boned in the Target parking lot. Mitch and his friends were okay (although, to this day, he is not over the fact that one of his friends—a girl—had to have a wound she'd sustained on her head stapled), but the Neon was totaled. Mitch was sited as "at fault" because he had looked toward the girl when she said, "Mitch! Look!" in order to take his photo and didn't see the car that hit him approaching from the left. Now, as it often goes with young drivers, the Neon had already sustained a variety of dents and dinks while being Mitch's "ride," and being that the Neon was the only car Kevin and I ever purchased without GAP insurance, it turned out we were upside-down on it about $500. In the community we lived in then, in Monument, Colorado, many people thought we were the meanest parents on earth when we didn't race out and purchase a new car for Mitch to drive. Instead, we sat him down and explained that since we had owned the Neon, he would need to pay the $500 we were upside-down, the $500 deductible, and then $1,000 to put down on another car—a car that would be for him to drive but that Kevin and I would own. I don't know if I've told you this before, but Kevin and I have the three wisest, most understanding, humble, and strong kids ever born! Therefore, Mitch agreed. He had been sited (even though the girl that hit him said it was her fault), had totaled a car that didn't belong to him, and was seventeen years old—old enough to take on the responsibility we had given him. Mitch worked that entire summer of 2007—worked very hard for a landscaper. Well, as summer began to wane, the start of Mitch's senior year was fast approaching, and we needed a third car so that Mitch could drive himself to school. So the Friday night before the Monday school was to start, Kevin and I went to bed with a plan to wake up and spend our Saturday searching for an appropriate teenager car for Mitch to drive to school. That night I had a dream. I dreamt that Kevin and I were on our way to buy a car for Mitch to drive. As we pulled into the car lot, I saw a used, canary-yellow Mustang sitting there.

"We should get that yellow car for Mitch," I suggested to Kevin in my dream.

"Why?" Kevin asked.

"Well, first of all, it's a Mustang...and Mitchel has always wanted a Mustang," I began to explain (again in my dream). "I think that if he had some pride in what he was driving—not too much pride, but some—maybe he would drive more carefully...you know, not dink and dent it up like he did the Neon."

"He has worked really hard this summer to pay off the Neon and save up," Kevin offered. "He's learned a very valuable lesson and has not once complained about the plan we suggested for making compensation. I think it would be a loving, trusting gesture on our part to get it. You know, show him that we do trust him and admire how hard he's worked."

"Yeah," I agreed. "And you know what else?"

"What?" Kevin prodded.

"There's no way anyone can miss that color of a car coming at them," I explained. "He'll be a lot more visible to other drivers. I think that's a good safety measure too."

In my dream Kevin agreed, and we purchased the used, canary-yellow Mustang.

Well, that was the end of my dream, and when we woke up the next morning, I just thought it was kind of strange. I didn't mention it to anyone, not even Kevin. As we were getting ready to leave, Mitch came in and handed the $1,000 he'd earned toward a down payment. It was the last of what he had earned. Poor kid. We felt awful taking it but had privately agreed that we needed to follow through with the plan. And so we accepted Mitch's hard-earned cash and headed into Colorado Springs. Kevin knew of a Ford car lot he'd planned on going to first. We had discussed getting something comparable to the Dodge Neon—like a Ford Focus or something. However, as we pulled up to the car lot area, we groaned when we saw that all the car lots were having some sort of sale thing going on. They had everything roped off to funnel drivers down a long corridor that all the car lots fed off of—and lining the roped-off area were about a million car salespeople! It was very overwhelming and not at all something two introverted parents wanted to entangle ourselves in.

"I'm not getting stuck in all of this," Kevin said. "But you know, there's a Kia dealership just up here a ways. Let's look there. They don't sell used cars, but Kia has some compact options. Let's just go look, okay?"

Disheartened by the long line of cars and salespeople we passed heading up to the Kia dealership, I was already stressed.

And then, the unthinkable happened. As we drove closer to the Kia dealership, I saw it! There in the front of the parking lot of the Kia dealership was parked a used, canary-yellow Mustang with a sticker in the window that said $8,899. Yes, my eyes nearly popped out of my head, and I thought, "Okay…I have to be imagining this!" But I wasn't! It really was there! At that point I figured it was time to tell Kevin about my dream—and so I did. And do you know what he said after I'd told him? He said, "Well, we better go look at it, then!"

We did more than just look at it: we purchased it! The super cool Mustang was only five years old and only had 20,000 miles on it. It had had only one owner and was in supreme condition. I will never, never in all my life forget the look on Mitch's face when we drove up in that car. He could not believe it! He could not believe we'd purchased what was, at that time, his dream wheels—that we were trusting him with it.

Oh, he took all kinds of heat from people. Parents who thought we were terrible for not racing out and purchasing him a new car after the Neon was totaled made snide remarks to him like, "Oh, so you wreck a car and your parents just go out and buy you a sportscar, huh?" We had warned Mitch that people would do that—and were sad when they actually did! But I think the one moment that kind of helped Mitch and Kevin and I snicker with delight was when, at the end of his senior year, we opened his yearbook to see that our little, used, canary-yellow Mustang had been chosen as one of the top three "coolest rides" in the high school! What made it even better was a huge portion of the kids who attended Mitch's high school drove brand-new Porsches, BMWs, and Hummers. And, no, I'm not kidding about that. There were kids and parents who were livid that Mitch's yellow Mustang had won such an honor!

Anyway, to make a long story longer, that Mustang served Mitch very well for the rest of his years at home. And when, at age nineteen, Mitch left to serve a two-year mission for our church, the yellow Mustang passed on to our youngest son, Trent. By the time Trent was driving the Mustang, we had moved back to New Mexico, where Mustangs were a dime a dozen. But the fact that our Mustang (our boys call her "The Beast") was a 2002 canary yellow made it a standout, and it owned as much fame for Trent in Rio Rancho, New Mexico, as it had for Mitch in Monument, Colorado. Now, here we are, eleven years later, and The Beast is still alive. Since Trent was our last kid to leave the nest, he took the yellow Mustang with him when he moved out and then got married. We get the biggest kick out of seeing our little five-foot-two daughter-in-law (Trent's wife) drive up in The Beast and step out. It's adorable. Furthermore, Mitch, Trent, and I—and even my daughter, Sandy—have a profound affection for The Beast and her history. I asked Kevin what we would do when Trent and Karli decide to upgrade to a newer, more family-convenient car. What would we do with the canary-yellow Mustang that has served our family so diligently and well? He says we'll sell it, of course—because I can't keep it as just a big souvenir. I don't understand why both Kevin and Pike's dad think that our sweet, cherished Mustang is too big to be a souvenir. But being that neither of my boys is ready to give The Beast over to the junkyard or a stranger, I think we'll be able to keep it in the family awhile longer. And either way, now you know why Pike drives an old canary-yellow Mustang!

Just for fun, I've included three photos of The Beast and my boys: 1. The Beast the day Kevin and I brought her home. 2. Mitch (wearing his camo Scooby Doo PJ bottoms, of course), sitting in

The Beast for the first time. 3. Trent and The Beast in May 2012—the last week of his senior year in high school.

Snippet #6—Or maybe an Addendum to Snippet #5. Our family operates with the emotion and attitude that inanimate objects are alive and have feelings too. How my kids and I feel about our Mustang, The Beast, is just one example. However, I am convinced that worries and love over and of objects is an inherited trait that we all got from my mom. Years ago, before her mind was lost to her completely, Mom was sitting with me while I was pinning a quilt. I had purchased a new box of pins and came across three or four pins that were not sharp on the tips and therefore that I couldn't use. I felt bad for the pins! After all, they weren't even going to have the chance to live outside their plastic box for very long, let alone nestle in some lovely, soft fabric. Well, as I found the dull-pointed pins, I laid them in front of my Mom, letting her know that I couldn't use them. When we were finished pinning the quilt and cleaning up the fabric scraps, I watched Mom pick up the discarded, imperfect pins and gently roll them up in a scrap of pretty fabric. "I'm sorry you didn't get to be in a quilt, little pins. I'm sorry that we have to just toss you away."

Yep, there we were, me and my mom, teary-eyed over a few dull-tipped pins that made it through quality control and into the store. At least Pike and Ambria get me—Pike with his own Mustang, Ambria with her little china dog! (And yes, the little china dog is based on one that I received as a very little girl from my Auntie. And yes, it sits in a very special, very protected, very old antique secretary where my grandbabies can gaze at it with wonder—and know that it's alive!) And Kevin thinks I can give up the Mustang without a struggle, without bawling my eyes out? He's nuts!

Snippet #7—Down in Albuquerque's North Valley, near where I grew up, nestled in a rather odd place, is the dreamy Victorian respite, the St. James Tearoom. Although I had heard of the St. James Tearoom before last year, it wasn't until September of last year that my daughter and I discovered its magical whimsy together! The tearoom is a place of wonder, where each month the owners and employees create a much-needed escape for patrons through themed high tea menus and décor. The very first time my daughter, Sandy, and I attended high tea at St. James, the theme was Harry Potter, and it was glorious! The three-tiered server was stacked high with delicious savories, breads, and sweets, each and every one bestowed with a Harry Potter-themed name. For instance, that month we enjoyed a tiny cordial glass filled with pumpkin juice; the glass itself had been chilled, and the rim dipped in sugar and nutmeg.

We also enjoy a House Elves' Savory Pudding and a Levitating Strawberry Trifle! In December, A Christmas Carol was the theme, and included Fezziwig's Fidget Pie. January's Tea in the Shire was one of our favorites to date and treated us to Sam's Roasted Vegetables and a Hobbiton Herb Roll among so many other delicious Hobbit yummies. In March we loved the Dublin's Fare menu, including the Beef and Ale Pot of Gold with Cheese Biscuit and the Country Apple Cake. And in April we experienced our favorite little tea sandwich (and our favorite thing to date!), which was the White Sands Hotel Chicken Salad in honor of the Anne of Green Gables theme! Now that's just the food! And as delicious, unique, and wonderful as it always is, it's the atmosphere in the private nooks and the two hours alone together spent quietly chatting and sipping herbal teas with names like Lavender Lace, Peach Promenade, and Daybreak in Martinique that settles our minds, soothes our very souls, and relaxes us! Each nook is small and intimate, decorated in a beautiful Victorian England theme, and named for and inspired by an English historical figure. Sandy and I have relished this time together as our own for nearly a year! I can't begin to tell you what it means to us as a mother and daughter to have that time to ourselves. It's truly an enchanting escape from the stresses of life! I've also taken one of my daughters-in-law for high tea there; Sandy and I are treating her to high tea at St. James' for her birthday soon. My sister is coming to visit this year, and I plan to whisk her away for a wondrous two hours, as well. Anyway, now you know whence came my inspiration for Miss Woodhouse's Tearoom in this book. And knowing Ambria as you now do, isn't it perfect that she chose a career that nestles her there? (If you'd like to peruse the St. James Tearoom photos and menus, or if you're ever in Albuquerque and have the chance to attend high tea there, just visit the St. James Tearoom on Facebook or visit www.stjamestearoom.com. It's truly an experience that will lift your spirits to cloud nine!)

Snippet #8—Have you ever worried that someone would see something personal you had in your purse or something the way Ambria worried Pike might somehow, some way, see the photo of him she'd been caching in her wallet when they met up after four years at Mancini's? Well, I think the majority of us have worried over something like that. But for those of you who never have—who perhaps have a better grip on possibilities and impossibilities—here's a little story for you, a real-life experience that mirrors Ambria's concern that night at Mancini's. (The name in this story has been changed to protect the wildly paranoid and innocent friend I experienced this with.)

So, there we were, me and Zelda. It was spring in Rexburg, Idaho, in 1984, and Zelda and I had skipped our morning Rick's College classes. Why? Because a serious and very secret mission was afoot. We had skipped classes so that we could walk to the drugstore in downtown Rexburg to purchase "equipment" (as my mother called them) or "supplies" (as my friend's mother called them). ("Equipment" and "supplies" are defined as tampons and sanitary napkins/pads. It's important that you know what we were on our way to the drugstore to purchase.)

At approximately nine a.m., Zelda and I entered the drugstore. Quickly we did some visual reconnaissance, which revealed to us that there was one other customer in the store (a WM—white male), one cashier (WF—white female), and one stockboy (also a WM). Although we were glad that we had only three other subjects to deal with, we were unsettled that two of them were male. You see, Zelda

175

never, ever purchased equipment/supplies in front of any male subjects! None!

We went on maneuvers at that point, feigning interest in hairspray and lipstick, until the WM customer finally paid the WF cashier for his purchases. It was an intense, high-stress situation—much like snipers experience while on twenty-four-hour shifts in war-torn countries.

Once the WM customer had exited the building, Zelda and I moved quickly—in standard two-by-two formation—to the equipment/supplies aisle of the drugstore. With the speed of lightning, I seized what I needed, and Zelda appropriated what she needed (tampons and panty liners—one box each for each of us), and we made a hasty retreat to the checkout area. Having reached our first line of defense, we plopped our equipment and supplies down on the counter in front of the cashier.

"I'll just pay for it all, and you can give me cash later," Zelda whispered to me. "We've got to get out of here before someone else comes in!"

"Roger that," I agreed—for although I was not as paranoid when buying equipment as Zelda was, I didn't want to risk losing her. Not on my watch.

The cashier began her process, and Zelda and I thought we were home free. And we would have been—*if* this had been taking place now, in the era of scanable barcodes, and not in 1984 where prices were placed on products with little white stickers so that the cashier could manually punch in the amount.

Lo and behold, Zelda had picked up the one box of tampons that did not have a white pricing label on it.

"Leonard? Will you do a price check for me on a twenty-four count box of tampons please?" the cashier hollered across the store.

(P.S. Leonard's name has also been changed to protect his anonymity in this story.)

For a moment, I thought Zelda and I were standing in the Korean demilitarized zone and that Zelda had been hit by enemy fire. As her face turned the deepest shade of red I have ever witnessed on a human being, I quickly studied her from head to toe to make sure she hadn't been wounded. Nope. She was just mortified—close to passing out—but only mortified. She'd make it out. I'd make sure of that. Even if I had to carry her.

"Three ninety-nine on that box of tampons," Leonard shouted from the back of the store.

As Zelda struggled to breathe, I helped her hand the cash total for our equipment and supplies to the cashier. Expeditiously, we shoved our supplies and equipment into a backpack that Zelda had carried with her.

Bidding a kind adieu to the WF cashier, Zelda and I sprinted from the drugstore and out into the protection of the street, where no one knew what we had just purchased.

Embarrassed and out of breath, Zelda and I began the long (UPHILL) trek back to our dormitory. It was only a couple of miles, but being that spring in Rexburg is more like winter in Colorado, we discovered that the temperature was dropping rapidly and a heavy snow had begun to fall.

The situation wasn't new or even unfamiliar to Zelda and me. We'd gone grocery shopping downtown a month or so before, having arrived at the store when the temperature was maybe thirty degrees. But we had found that, by the time we finished, the temperature was dropping like a lead balloon. By the time we made it home, our hair was frosted and brittle and would break off if you tried to snap it, and our earrings were frozen in our ears with a little pad of ice around the opening.

Therefore, we were, understandably, unsettled by the sudden change in the weather. Still, we had accomplished our mission thus far and were confident we could make it home before we succumbed to hypothermia.

As we continued trudging up the steep, steep hill that led to our dorm (which sat on the very top of the hill, mind you), a familiar car pulled up alongside us. I instantly recognized the white, 1970's-era sportscar. It belonged to a guy I knew, Steve (and that's his real name).

Steve rolled down the window and smiling asked, "Hey! You guys want a ride? I'm on my way up there now."

Before I could unclench my chattering teeth and open my mouth to accept Steve's thoughtful, gracious offer of safety from the elements, Zelda piped out, "Oh no! We're just fine! We're getting our exercise! But thanks anyway!"

"Are you sure?" Steve asked, looking at me like I'd lost my marbles.

"Oh, we're sure," Zelda assured him. "But thanks so much!"

"Okay, then," Steve said with a shrug. "See you later."

As Steve sped off in his warm, fast sportscar, I looked to Zelda and asked, "Why did you tell him no? It's freezing out here, and we still have so far to walk!"

Zelda looked back at me with a puzzled expression indicating she could not understand why I didn't understand why she had not accepted the ride.

"Well, because he might have asked us what was in my backpack," she explained.

I stood there in the freezing cold not only astonished but also thoroughly amused. Zelda had refused Steve's offer of giving us a ride home because she was afraid he would ask her what was in her backpack? Now, we all know that Steve never would've asked; nobody would've asked! No one would've cared, right? But even if he had asked, what was he going to say? "You guys got tampons and panty liners in the backpack or what?" No, he wouldn't have. Seriously, if Steve had been weird or nosy enough to ask what Zelda was packing, all she would've needed to say was, "Oh, just equipment and supplies," right? It's not like he would've kept pressing her until she had to say the "T" word (*tampon*).

To be utterly truthful, you have no idea how many times that story has given me the giggles, enriched my fond memories of Zelda, and just plain made me happy. And so, now that you understand exactly why Ambria shoved her purse under her chair at Mancini's out of fear that Pike would somehow know his photo was in her wallet, you also know from whence I drew the inspiration for that little tidbit in this book.

Snippet #9—Pike's cinnamon toothpicks. I *love* cinnamon toothpicks! I grew up getting them at the candy store or convenience store, but they seem hard to find these days. Years ago I began making my own. Here's the recipe if you're interested! One thing to not do: do *not* store them in plastic jars or bags. Only store them in glass or in little bags or envelopes you've made out of waxed paper.

Supplies (Not the Feminine Kind) and Ingredients:
Round toothpicks
A wide-mouth glass jar for soaking

Some sort of glass jar or waxed paper bags for storage
Cinnamon oil (I like cinnamon bark oil)
Paper towels
Paper plates

Pour cinnamon oil to cover the bottom of your wide-mouthed glass jar. Place the toothpicks in the oil in the jar. Make sure the toothpicks are all submerged in the oil. Seal the jar with its lid, and let the toothpicks soak overnight.

The next day, place paper towels on a paper plate. Take the toothpicks out of the jar, spread them on the paper towels, and allow them to dry. If they are not dry in a few hours, dab them with another paper towel to remove excess cinnamon oil. You might need to place them on new paper towels—the idea being that they are dry once they don't leave oil marks on the paper towel.

Store your toothpicks in a glass vile or jar of some kind, or make little bags out of waxed paper.

Note: These can be pretty hot, so try one yourself before giving them to kids, okay? If you feel they are too strong for you, you can soak your toothpicks for a lesser amount of time (i.e., only a few hours as opposed to overnight).

Snippet #10—Ambria tastes like cinnamon. Okay, you know how Pike tastes Ambria's hair and swears it tastes like cinnamon? Well, that inspiration also came from my husband, Kevin. I caught him sniffing our dog's head one day. Seriously sniffing it like we women sniff the heads of new babies, right? I asked him what he was doing, and he answered, "He smells just like maple syrup! He really does! Sniff him!" Well, Charlie smells good—like a puppy's sweet little tummy to me, not a full-grown dog. But the scent of maple syrup escapes me when I sniff his head. Still, to Kevin, Charlie smells like maple syrup. And to Pike, Ambria's hair tastes like cinnamon. So who am I to argue?

Snippet #11—Madison's second attempt at Pike. I had a roommate in college who drove me and my other roommates crazy! (Let's call her Helga.) AND she had a diehard crush on Kevin. Mind you, Kevin and I were already engaged when she met and crushed on him. But that didn't stop her! She was always finding reasons to call him, write him little notes and things. She would leave little notes like, *Kevy…our sink is clogged. Do you think you could fix it for us? Love and Kisses, Helga!* In fact, one time I had made a candy gram for Kevin (you might have to Google that if you were born after 1995), and my other roommate and I had huffed it up the hill to his apartment in Rexburg, Idaho, so that we could have it waiting there for him when he got home from class. Well, lo and behold, who did we find waiting at Kevin's apartment with Kevin's roommates for Kevin to return home? That's right, Helga!!!! I forget what her excuse for being there was, but it was lame. She backed off after a while but made my life as miserable as she could because she wasn't able to snatch Kevin away from me. It still makes me mad to think about it all these years later. Of course, she wasn't my sister—but still!

Snippet #12—Kevin quotes in this book. I know I'll take some heat from some readers for Pike even thinking the term "didn't give a rat's ass"—but it's one of Kevin's phrases that he uses when ranting that just totally crack up me, my kids, and in-law kids. The other phrase he uses a lot that I love because it's a good way to just start figuring out how to fix any problem that arises, is "I'll just spit it out and clean it up later." It's perfect! AND it works! If you ever had trouble putting your thoughts into words, just spit out your thoughts and organize them later. That is, of course, if you have a tact filter. Don't spit them out before your tact filter is engaged, okay?

Snippet #13—Mr. Rogers' "It's You I Like." Since I conceived Ambria's discomfort with her bosom was to be a running theme in this book, Mr. Rogers' song "It's You I Like" has been running through my head nearly nonstop. I so love the message of that song! It's so perfect! The melody is soft and soothing as well. It's a song we should all sing to our kids and grandkids, you know? (I'm going to start tomorrow!) It should be a part of our lives today much more than it is. I wanted, so very badly, to have Pike romantically sing that song to Ambria that night in the pool—maybe even put a few of his own "likes" about her into it. But when we researched how much it would cost for permission to use even one line of the lyrics to it, *if* they even gave permission, I realized what a big dog Mr. Rogers' songs really are! Even to ask permission was pricey beyond belief! Other than J.K. Rowling, Stephen King, or someone like that, I doubt anyone could afford to quote his song lyrics in a book! Still, it's a beautiful, beautiful song, and in so many ways. Furthermore, I agree with Pike—"This world would be a much better place if people still raised their kids on *Mr. Rogers' Neighborhood* and *Sesame Street.*"

Snippet #14—The Blue Tutu Incident of 1970 or '71. I'll make this as short as I can because it is an uncomfortable memory. When my friend "Betty" and I were in first grade, we were somehow signed up to perform in the school talent show. We took dance classes together and had recently performed in our recital—a snappy little number choreographed to "The Glow-Worm." I was pretty excited when I discovered that the pretty sky-blue tutu that I had received to wear for the recital was actually mine to keep! Well, the day arrived for the talent show, and nervous as we were, Betty and I were confident we would do well. After all, we'd already performed the routine at the recital. So what could possibly go wrong at the school talent show? Our routine started off beautifully! There we were, "glow little glow worming" our little hearts out (and perfectly, if I do say so myself). And then it happened—the worst, most embarrassing thing that could've happened. My hands on my hips as I danced, I looked over to see how Betty was doing—and that's when I noticed it. Our tutu tops were secured by two little ribbons that tied at the back of our necks—you know, like some aprons do. As I watched in horror—all the while never missing a step—Betty's tutu top began to slide down! Her tie ribbons had obviously come untied, and before I knew it, the entire bodice of Betty's tutu had flopped down over her tummy! Everything from the waist up was revealed!!!! It was horrifying! And I did not know what to do. I just continued to "glow little glow worm," even as I was mortified for us both. Poor Betty! I think I suffered some PTSD from that incident, because I have a memory like an elephant (ask any member of my family, some of whom hate the fact—ha ha!), and I cannot for the life of me remember what happened! Did Betty and I finish the dance? Did Betty's mom race out and save her from further humiliation? I have no idea what happened! Beyond the initial memory of poor Betty being a topless little glow worm for a bit, I cannot remember what happened. Definitely a PTSD repressed memory—I hope it stays that way! (Just for fun, here's a photo of my own daughter wearing my infamous blue tutu. She's icing

Christmas sugar cookies, of course. What else would you expect a six-year-old to do in a tutu if there's no glow worm dancing to do? I also have a photo of my youngest son wearing the tutu at age two and a half years…thanks to his sister. But because I love him, I chose not to include that one, wink wink!)

To my hero and inspiration…
Kevin from Heaven!

ABOUT THE AUTHOR

Marcia Lynn McClure's intoxicating succession of novels, novellas, and e-books—including *Shackles of Honor*, *The Windswept Flame*, *A Crimson Frost*, and *The Bewitching of Amoretta Ipswich*—has established her as one of the most favored and engaging authors of true romance. Her unprecedented forte in weaving captivating stories of western, medieval, regency, and contemporary amour void of brusque intimacy has earned her the title "The Queen of Kissing."

Marcia, who was born in Albuquerque, New Mexico, has spent her life intrigued with people, history, love, and romance. A wife, mother, grandmother, family historian, poet, and author, Marcia Lynn McClure spins her tales of splendor for the sake of offering respite through the beauty, mirth, and delight of a worthwhile and wonderful story.

BIBLIOGRAPHY

A Bargained-For Bride

Beneath the Honeysuckle Vine

A Better Reason to Fall in Love

The Bewitching of Amoretta Ipswich

Born for Thorton's Sake

The Chimney Sweep Charm

A Cowboy for Christmas

A Crimson Frost

Daydreams

Desert Fire

Divine Deception

Dusty Britches

The Fragrance of Her Name

The General's Ambition

A Good-Lookin' Man

The Haunting of Autumn Lake

The Heavenly Surrender

The Highwayman of Tanglewood

Indebted Deliverance

Kiss in the Dark

Kissing Cousins

The Light of the Lovers' Moon

Love Me

The Man of Her Dreams

Midnight Masquerade

The Object of His Affection

An Old-Fashioned Romance

One Classic Latin Lover, Please

The Pirate Ruse

The Prairie Prince
The Rogue Knight
Romance at the Christmas Tree Lot
Romance in a Winter Wonderland
Romance in Sleepy Hollow
The Romancing of Evangeline Ipswich
Romance with a Side of Green Chile
Romance with the Summer Son
Saphyre Snow
The Secret Bliss of Calliope Ipswich
Shackles of Honor
The Stone-Cold Heart of Valentine Briscoe
Sudden Storms
Sweet Cherry Ray
Take a Walk with Me
The Tide of the Mermaid Tears
The Time of Aspen Falls
To Echo the Past
The Touch of Sage
The Trove of the Passion Room
The Unobtainable One
Untethered
The Visions of Ransom Lake
Weathered Too Young
The Whispered Kiss
With a Dreamboat in a Hammock
The Windswept Flame
The Wolf King

www.ingramcontent.com/pod-product-compliance
Lightning Source LLC
Chambersburg PA
CBHW060438180626

46817CB00007B/2885